THE IRON STIRRUP

In New Mexico, highwaymen rob a stage of a bullion box. No one knows where the ill-gotten money is, or who has it, but one by one the highwaymen show up in Culleyville. Al Burton, the whip driving the stage, was shot in the hip and returned to Culleyville to recuperate. Soon there is a murder to be solved and the money still hasn't been found. Then a Pinkerton agent arrives with many questions to ask. Now the fat is truly in the fire!

Books by Russ Thompson
in the Linford Western Library:

SADDLER'S WELLS

RUSS THOMPSON

THE IRON STIRRUP

Complete and Unabridged

LINFORD
Leicester

First published in Great Britain in 1999 by
Robert Hale Limited
London

First Linford Edition
published 2000
by arrangement with
Robert Hale Limited
London

British Library CIP Data

Thompson, Russ, *1916* –
    The iron stirrup.—Large print ed.—
Linford western library
1. Western stories
2. Large type books
I. Title
813.5′4 [F]

ISBN 0–7089–5793–5

Published by
F. A. Thorpe (Publishing)
Anstey, Leicestershire

Set by Words & Graphics Ltd.
Anstey, Leicestershire
Printed and bound in Great Britain by
T. J. International Ltd., Padstow, Cornwall

This book is printed on acid-free paper

1

Six Miles Out and Back — Twice

She had wanted a larger house. He had said 'someday' and the years rolled by until that fierce blizzard when they had been snowbound for twelve days and she had been taken down and died. The doctor came out when the weather permitted it and said she would have died anyway, housebound or not, but for a long time her husband lived with the guilt of not attempting to get her to town where the doctor lived.

The second year their son left home and that hurt his father too. They'd had a terrible argument. Things had been said that ate at the father.

As the Mexicans said, *tiempo pasar*, time passes. He really had no intention of building that larger, elegant house and that ate at him too.

They had migrated from Missouri, had staked their claim and worked fifteen hours a day. What wore her out toughened him. He could have built that house which was one thing his son William had said, but no, every penny went into more land, more cattle. The bitterest part was now; he had money, plenty of it. His cattle ranged over dozens of miles of deeded land, and now when he went to the log house he had built that first year he was the only one in it. In his own way he was satisfied, more than satisfied. He could ride out blizzards, droughts, the winds which his part of New Mexico was noted for. He put the Mexicans to making wood in summer with which he cooked and kept warm in winter.

He didn't talk much to himself but he talked to horses, an occasional old sick cow.

His name was Travis McCulley but he had dropped the 'Mac' years ago. To the folks who knew him he was plain Travis Culley. His father wouldn't have approved. He'd emigrated from the 'auld sod' fifty years earlier. Father and son shared many things, uncompromising dedication to hard work, long hours, loyalty. It was the loyalty that killed the father. At some insignificant creek in the Carolinas he had caught one through the head; they wrapped him in the Confederacy's battle flag and buried him where the ground was soft beside that little creek.

They had gotten along well enough, the old man and his son Travis. They were enough alike to make that possible. They had differed over the girl Travis wanted to marry, the old man sized her up like a horse or a bull and had said she was too fine boned, too delicate for a pioneering existence and he had been right. That was something Travis never forgot.

She'd almost died birthing William.

Springtime arrived with warmth, budding flowers, calving cows and Travis sat in the rocker he'd made on the porch of the old log house breathing

3

deeply of spring's fragrance and thinking how things could have been if he hadn't been so much like his father.

He would visualize how that elegant big house would have looked. He was doing that one early May afternoon when he saw the rider coming in a slow lope from the direction of Culleyville. Travis owned most of the place; when folks wanted to name the town for him he thanked them and granted permission without showing any pleasure about it.

There were neighbours, mostly miles distant like his town. It was six miles from his ranch yard to Culleyville. He watched the loping horseman with indifferent concern; he had few friends and fewer visitors.

The rider dropped down to a kidney-jolting trot the last half-mile, entered the yard, passed the outbuildings and the large log barn and walked his horse in the direction of the man gently rocking on the porch.

He was Sherman Kandelin, town marshal at Culleyville, the only lawman for a hundred miles in any direction.

He nodded toward the rocking chair, dismounted, looped both reins at the tie rack and fished in a pocket as he crossed to the porch.

Travis nodded in silence until the town marshal handed him a folded paper. He stopped rocking long enough to open the paper and smooth it flat with both work-scarred big hands.

The town marshal looked for something to sit on, found nothing and went to hook one haunch over the peeled-log porch railing.

Travis read the paper twice. The watching lawman saw his jaw ripple, that was all before he handed the paper back, looked Kandelin in the eye when he spoke.

'Where'd you get that thing, Sherm?'

Kandelin was refolding the paper before depositing it in the same pocket from which it had come as he answered.

5

'It come with the post yestiddy morning. The store-keeper Frank Christy brought it over to the jailhouse . . . Travis?'

'It might not be William. He didn't look a lot different from other fellers his age, an' all.'

The town marshal shifted on his unyielding perch. 'It's him. I sent a wire to Deming. They wired back last night, late. He give them your name as his pa.'

Travis rocked through a long silence, gazing dead ahead over land he owned as far as a person could see. 'Why would he do a thing like that?'

Kandelin beat dust off his hat before answering. 'I'd guess for money; why else do they stop stages?'

'Wire them for the details, Sherm.'

'I'll do that.' Kandelin stood up looking at the older man. 'I thought you'd ought to know.'

'I'm obliged, Sherman.'

'That's all, Travis?'

The older man's steel-blue eyes went to the town marshal. 'What'd you

6

expect? I haven't seen William nor heard from him in ten, twelve years. Sherm, all a man can do is give them his name. When they get as old as he is that's the onliest thing they share. He left here. He could've stayed; I needed him.'

Kandelin nodded, went out to his horse, swung astride and left the yard in a slow lope, his back as straight as a ramrod. He hadn't expected the coldness, but he told his horse he should have.

'That old bastard. I'm not makin' an excuse. He shouldn't have robbed that stage, but for Chris'sake folks stand by their own. This'll be all over the territory like wildfire. Travis isn't well liked. Folks'll like spreadin' this story. They'll say like father, like son.'

The horse had six miles to go before he'd get a bait of hay and maybe half a tin of rolled barley. He could lope the full distance without showing a sweat.

Sherman Kandelin was right. Someone over at the store had seen the

Wanted dodger. By the time Kandelin put up his animal and went to the jailhouse, Culleyville's folks knew as much as the town marshal knew and had begun the variety of verbal embroidery such things gathered with the retelling.

He was braced at least four times about the old man's son being a damned highwayman. Kandelin denied nothing. He left folks with the impression he did not want to talk about it.

He went up to the bank which was where he drew his monthly pay and the young fellow who had been imported from Denver to run the bank nailed him as the clerk was counting and recounting the thirty dollars. His name was Alfred Lewis. He slapped Kandelin on the back and said, 'Culleyville's got a new reason for bein' known. The home of William Culley, replacement for Jesse James.'

Sherman pocketed the money, looked the banker straight in the eyes and said, 'You been here three years, Alfred. I'd

8

be a mite careful about shootin' off your mouth if I was you.'

Lewis's congenial mood died. He faced the clerk behind his steel framework and said, 'What's eating him?'

The clerk's reply was given curtly. 'Good advice Mr Lewis.'

Over at the telegraph office the man wearing a green eyeshade read the message, picked up the coins and was expressionless when he said, 'If they answer it might be late afternoon, or maybe tomorrow.'

Sherm bypassed the saloon, went to the eatery and had a meal. There were other diners, including a pair of Mexican ranch hands who garbled in their native language and laughed. They were careful not to look in the town marshal's direction. The other diners nodded and concentrated on their dinner. They had been talking up a storm before the lawman had walked in. After that they did not so much as ask the caféman for refilled coffee cups.

Sherman lingered at the jailhouse until after dark. The telegraph man did not appear so he went to his room at the rooming-house and turned in.

He had finished breakfast and was at his desk in the jailhouse when the telegrapher walked in carrying a yellow piece of paper which he put on the desk, said, 'Rain's comin',' and departed.

Sherman thumbed his hat back, leaned and pursed his mouth as he read. The robbery had happened about two miles north of a hamlet called Glorioso. The marshal softly nodded: one of those little hamlets that New Mexico had hundreds of. The coach had a gun guard. He winged one of the highwaymen. The other two reached their horses and ran. The wounded outlaw was captured and questioned. He had revealed the names of his companions. Arthur Holding and William Culley. They had cornered Culley in a dry wash where he walked out and let the posseman capture him.

10

There was one short final line to the telegram. The gun guard had come through, but the whip had been shot in the hip.

Sherm decided not to ride out and show the telegram to Travis. He would ride twelve miles, six out and six back, and all he'd get for his trouble would be more of the same he had gotten the day before.

Someone, possibly the telegrapher, helped word get around what had been in the town marshal's telegraphed enquiry. It was enough, especially the part about the whip getting shot. People right away jumped to the conclusion that the shooter was William Culley, not the armed men riding with him.

At the saloon, the marshal said there was no proof the old man's son had shot the whip or anyone else. His annoyance bordering on anger stifled the talk until he left, then it was resumed and someone said Sherman Kandelin taking the side of an

11

outlaw didn't fit well with the badge he wore.

A widow woman named Lisbeth Deane stopped by the jailhouse as the marshal was ready to get fed over at Culleyville's only eatery. Kandelin put his hat back atop the desk, motioned toward a chair and smiled. He had known her husband; he had been killed in a mine explosion in northern Arizona several years earlier. She kept body and soul together by doing whatever she could to live. That included sometimes washing dishes at the eatery, sewing for local womenfolk and house cleaning.

She was a young thirty-three with amber eyes, the complexion to match and the most handsome smile in Culleyville.

She had a scrap of information that kept Sherm Kandelin motionless and silent at his desk.

'Do you remember my brother, Marshal?'

Kandelin nodded. Her brother had

driven stage throughout the territory; had boarded with his widowed sister. Sherm said, 'Al Burton. What about him?'

'He was the whip on that stage down south whom Will Culley shot.'

'Al . . . ?'

She nodded. 'I received a letter from him this morning. He got hit in the . . . upper leg. They told him William Culley shot him.'

Sherman leaned back off the desk without taking his gaze off the woman. 'Where is he now, Lisbeth?'

'In a hospital in Deming. Why I came by, I can't afford the telegraph, I will write him a letter. Marshal?'

'Yes'm.'

'Does Will's father know?'

'He knows, I showed him the Wanted dodger.'

'Would he want me to say anything to William?'

Sherman looked out the little barred front wall window and back before answering. He was thinking of his last meeting with Travis Culley. 'I don't know, Lisbeth.'

She showed a slight wintry smile. 'I understand, but he's the old man's son, and he's in trouble.'

Sherm rocked forward, locked his hands together and said, 'I'll ride out there.'

Her smile widened. 'I know it's asking a lot. I'd go but I can't afford to hire a horse.' She went as far as the roadway door before facing him and saying, 'They're close kin, Sherman. I know Travis Culley is as cold-blooded as they come, but his wife loved the ground William walked on. Shouldn't he do something for her sake?'

He went over to the door. 'I said I'll go out there.'

'I'll make supper for you when you get back. Is that all right?'

He considered the flawless complexion with the almost golden eyes and told her he'd get back as quickly as he could, watched her turn southward on

14

the plankwalk and gently closed the door.

He would have to make haste. The last time he'd ridden out there and back he had started earlier and hadn't got back before just shy of dusk.

At the livery barn where he kept his horse he rigged out the animal himself, exchanged as few words as possible with the liveryman and left town at a dead walk for a mile, then broke over into a trot and by the time he'd kept at that gait long enough he boosted over into a slow lope and held to it until he could make out the Culley buildings.

He didn't have to ride that last mile and a half. Travis and a Mexican who worked for him were down on their knees delivering a hung-up calf, the first for the heifer and did not look up even after Kandelin stopped, dismounted and watched.

He had worked other folk's cattle before hiring on as a town marshal so what he saw didn't bother him. He too had delivered hung-ups.

The Mexican hadn't rolled up his sleeves and they were discoloured and wet. Travis worked with no thought for anything but getting the calf out alive. His old saddle horse knew exactly what to do when the old man raised his right arm. It took three backward steps and stopped.

The Mexican, a slightly overweight older man, said something in Spanish and rocked back to laugh. Travis also rocked back but not for long. He pulled the slimy-wet baby up to its mother's face and left it. All three men waited and watched. The heifer was soaked with sweat. She smelled the calf and began licking it.

Travis did something that startled the town marshal. He said something in Spanish and slapped the Mexican on the back.

He used a large old blue bandanna to dry his hands and, as he did this, he looked at Kandelin. He finished wiping and went to his horse. 'Ride back with me,' he told the marshal and didn't look back.

They were about halfway when the older man spoke again, without looking at the man riding with him. 'William, isn't it?'

'Travis, do you remember a young feller named Al Burton around town a few years back?'

Travis bobbed his head. 'What about him?'

'William shot him during the stage hold-up.'

The older man turned his head. 'They were in it together?'

'No, Burton was the whip. There was a gun guard. He shot one of Will's companions. There were three highwaymen, Will an' two others. One of them got shot. William's in the Deming jail, Al Burton is in the hospital.'

'How do you know all this? Tie up at the rack; I'll get us something to drink.'

Sherm couldn't resist. As Travis reached the porch he sarcastically said,

'You ever heard of a thing called a telegraph?'

Travis's back was to Kandelin as he entered the house so the marshal couldn't see the splotches of colour in the older man's face.

Travis returned with a pitcher, two tin cups and some peppermints. They made tepid water taste cold. He filled both cups, handed one to his visitor and sat in the only chair, blew out a ragged breath and said, 'Son of a bitch! Did he have to shoot someone? Bad enough robbin' a stage. Where did you say he was?'

'In Deming.' Sherm said no more until he'd cheeked the peppermint and emptied the cup.

Travis spoke sharply without raising the cup. 'I know that country down there. They'll hang him.'

Sherm refilled his cup but did not raise it. 'Do you know a woman in town named Lisbeth Deane?'

'I know her. Pretty as a picture. Lost her husband in Arizona some time back. What about her?'

'She's sister to Al Burton. He sent her a letter from down there.'

The older man also drained and refilled his cup. 'I never could understand why she didn't remarry. She's as pretty as — '

'She's afraid for her brother.'

'Is she? How bad was he shot? William shot him! They used to ride all over hell together. Maybe he didn't see him good.'

Sherman let that pass; in a hold-up faces don't matter, guns do. 'She didn't say this to me, straight out, but if you could help her brother . . . '

Travis pushed his legs out and crossed them at the ankles. It wasn't a rousing success, he hadn't removed his spurs.

'Help her brother? An' get my son hung doin' it?'

'Travis, he asked for it.'

The older man emptied his second cupful, flung the dregs aside and started gently rocking. For a while they sat in

19

shade and silence.

Eventually Sherm arose as he said, 'I got to get back before dusk.'

Travis said, 'Set down, damn it!'

The marshal remained standing, but made no move to leave the porch. Culley looked up at him. 'Why in hell should I? All right, I'll do what I can for young Burton but I owe William nothing. You go back an' tell her that.' As Travis arose he shifted his gaze so that he was no longer considering Sherm Kandelin.

'Tell her she's welcome out here any time she wants. Now you better get a-horseback if you expect to get home in time for supper.'

2

One Man's World

Travis Culley very seldom hired extra rangemen, but he did keep one man year round. His name was Felice Obregon. He had a family somewhere in Mexico and routinely sent them money. He actually needed very little for himself. He had the whole bunkhouse to himself most of the time. It had been his home under the arrangement with Travis and they got along remarkably well. Travis had never learned Spanish and Felice had given up the struggle about learning good English. He got along; Travis caught him up over the years. They understood each other, but Felice's English was difficult for others to understand.

Felice was loyal to Travis. The Culley holdings were his world. He only visited town when Travis hitched up the wagon.

Felice had come to the ranch as a half-starved youth of about seventeen. Travis's wife had taken him in. He had been there ever since, something like fifteen years.

Every town in New Mexico had a Mex town, commonly separate from *gringo* town. That's the way it had been since time out of mind. It still was that way. When Felice's friends in Mex town wanted to visit they were discreet. Travis's disposition was widely known. It was the result of one of those discreet visitations from Mex town, at night after no light showed from the main house, that two *visitadores* came around the far side of the bunkhouse and scratched the door to tell Felice, Travis's son the outlaw had escaped from the law, something Felice told Travis in the morning.

Felice told Travis his son, the outlaw highwayman, had escaped from the Deming *juzgado*.

Travis listened without interrupting until Felice had told him all that he had learned the night before and Travis had filled two cups with black java and with his Mexican explored the possibilities of this news.

Felice had said *el jefe*'s son would make a run for it to get to the only home he had known from babyhood to manhood.

Travis shook his head. 'No. He won't come here. He dassen't. They'll look for him here.'

Felice disagreed but only to himself. Arguing with his employer achieved the identical result as arguing with a mule.

When news of Travis's son having escaped from where he was being held down south became stale news in and around Culleyville local interest settled on something else, something closer to home.

Two cow outfits combined in their drive north. It was an annual event, a lucrative one for Culleyville's merchants not to mention the town's smithy, and the saloon and gambling parlour which was operated by Hiram Boyard, a florid individual with several elegant gold teeth who was addicted to cigars. Cattle drives had used the same bed ground since the first drive had come north. It was about two miles east of Culleyville.

The northbound stage driver had seen the cattle and the wagons making camp at Boomer Spring two days earlier, and from this bit of gossip Culleyville's residents knew the drive would reach the creekside easterly campground within five or six days.

Local stockmen including Travis Culley rode long hours pushing their cattle as far as was necessary to prevent an intermingling.

In town, Marshal Sherman Kandel made his customary sashay around town organizing volunteer possemen. For a fact the drovers were commonly decent-acting in town, but these were Texans so it paid to be prepared.

He was at Mex town settling a dispute between a pair of fired-up individuals over ownership of a rooster, when a slight man of indeterminate years and perfect white teeth which he showed in a wide smile at every opportunity, sidled up, caught the marshal's attention and jerked his head.

Sherm followed the man outside as far as a very ancient tree where his guide stopped, faced around and with an exaggerated conspiratorial attitude spoke in slightly more than a whisper.

'*Jefe*, he is with the *Tejanos*.'

Sherm frowned. 'Who? You mean the cattle drive?'

'*Si*, yes, he is one of the riders.'

'Who, damn it, is with the drive?'

'The son of *el mayor*.'

Sherm eyed the smaller man. Among the residents of Mex town Travis Culley was known as *el mayor*, the mayor.

'You mean young Culley? Will Culley?'

'Yes. He is among the riders.'

'How do you know this?'

The Mexican made a slight gesture with both hands as he answered. 'This is the *gringo* who often visited my sister. They visited often before he went away.'

'She told you it was him?'

'Yes. And who would know better?' As the marshal started to turn away the informer brushed his sleeve lightly. 'It is worth something this kind of truth?'

Sherm dug in a pocket, handed over several well-worn silver coins and went searching for the rooster owners. He found them at a table in the *cantina* drinking red wine and bargaining over how much one of them must pay for the servicing of the other one's hens. The question of ownership had been settled somewhere between the second and third glasses.

Later the marshal was at his jail-house, hat tipped, hands clasped atop the desk gazing dispassionately at an old Wanted poster tacked to the far wall.

He should have looked up the small man's sister and something else he should have done was to swear the woman and her brother to absolute secrecy. If someone even hinted at what Sherm had been told in Mex town . . . the whole area would be up in arms.

He went down to the smithy where the powerfully muscled proprietor was cross-tying someone's 1,200 pound mule, sat on a sooty bench and told the horse-shoer what he had been told by a scrawny Mexican.

The marshal and the blacksmith had been friends, more than just friends, since Sherm had arrived in the territory years back.

They exchanged greetings as the smith ran a hand down the backbone of the mule, told it what would happen if it bit or kicked him and went to work as though only he and the mule were in his shop.

He was bent over with a hind foot cradled ready to pull the hind shoe when he said, 'If it's true Will has turned bad, he'll likely look me up. I beat him at poker an' pedro every time

27

we set down . . . Sherm?'

'What?'

'You come down here to see if I'd ride with you?'

Kandelin considered his friend in that bent-over position as he answered. 'He was hell on wheels even before he went to stoppin' stages for a livin'.'

'Sherm, who else knows he might be comin' back?'

'Damned few, but it'll spread.'

The smith let the hoof slide off, straightened up with a grimace and held the mule shoe where the town marshal could see it. 'Tell me somethin', Sherm; why did Gawd make mules' feet different from horses's feet?'

Kandelin ignored the shoe and the question. He went as far as the roadway door before speaking again. 'You goin' with me or not?'

'Where's the drive?'

'South-east, maybe near Cockburn Rocks.'

'Two days' ride. I just close up an' go

horsebackin' two days to maybe find the drive an' just as maybe find out Will's not with it . . . I run a business here.'

When the smith leaned to fit the mule shoe for size, the town marshal was gone. The smith looked around at the mule. 'He never could stand a little teasin'. Now you rabbit-eared, ugly bastard, you so much as look like you want to bite my rear end when I bend over an' I'll make saddle-bags out of your hide.'

Sherm Kandelin left town riding west with the day still young. He didn't lope this time. He really didn't care whether Travis knew, or not. Mex town informants hadn't always carried genuine tales, but this time Sherm thought it likely this one had.

Men who straddled horses for as much as ten to twelve hours a day could be relied upon to be at home if they expected visitors.

Travis wasn't at his home place. Felice said he had ridden to town to see the banker. He invited the marshal to wait; by Felice's calculation, since Travis had left before sunrise he should be returning directly.

It was a good surmise. Sherm was sitting on the porch in the old man's rocker when Felice whistled from the barn and pointed.

Travis was coming ahead of a light skiff of dust. When he entered the yard and Felice appeared to take the horse, Travis said, 'How long's the law been settin' over there?'

Felice shrugged. 'Hour, a little more maybe.'

Sherm did not leave the chair nor offer his hand as the older man came up onto the porch. Travis said, 'Barely missed you. Somethin' on your mind? You're settin' in my chair.'

Sherm did not stop gently rocking nor did he arise so the chair's owner could use it.

He said, 'Will is with the drovers comin' up from down south.'

Travis blew out a breath. 'How do

you know that?'

'From someone over in Mex town. Travis . . . ?'

'I'm a sight older'n you are an' I been horsebackin' since sun-up an' my butt's sore.'

Sherm left the chair, went to lean on a peeled log stringer and went to work fashioning a smoke without looking at the older man.

Travis sat down and began to gently rock. He looked eastward, ignoring his visitor, when he said, 'He won't come here.'

Sherm lit up. 'I think he will.'

'What am I supposed to do about it?'

'Send Felice to let me know when he's here.'

The old man rocked and squinted easterly. 'He won't come here. Them drives don't lie over much anyway. Whoever told you he'd be with this bunch more'n likely made it up.'

'Suppose it's the truth an' suppose he comes out here.'

Travis stopped rocking and turned

his head. 'All right. But I won't promise you a damned thing.'

Travis stood up. Sherm nodded flintily and left the porch in the direction of the barn. Travis watched him bring his animal outside before mounting it, and head in the direction of town.

Felice came around the south-west corner of the barn smiling.

Travis turned on him. 'Listenin' again, wasn't you? Someday you're goin' to get your head blown off . . . you heard what he said?'

'*Si*, yes, I heard.'

'I want you to go to Mex town an' find out if William is really among them herders from the south.'

Felice was agreeable, mostly because since he owned no horse of his own he rarely visited friends in Mex town.

Travis went inside, fumbled with a whiskey bottle, filled a shot glass and returned to the porch, to the rocker, before downing it. The last place on earth his outlaw son would visit would be the house where he had been born and lived until they'd had their violent argument.

Travis raised the little jolt glass, held it aloft in some kind of salute and remained on the porch until he saw Felice coming, then he arose and wagged his head. Felice had come to them as a youngster. Travis had drummed into him how to care for animals and how to sit a saddle.

He hadn't learned. Even when Felice had been younger and carried less weight he didn't sit a horse well.

Travis went inside, put the little glass where it belonged and returned to the porch as Felice was leading his horse into the barn to be cared for.

Travis waited.

As Felice crossed the yard to the porch he called ahead in Spanish, which annoyed the older man who, except for a few words, had never learned the language, and called back, 'In English. What the hell's wrong with you . . . use English.'

Felice pulled off his old hat when he came to the porch's edge. 'He isn't there. No one knows if he is with the cattle, but they will find out and let me know.'

Travis said, '*Gracias*. Now go wash. I can smell you from here.'

Travis usually made sweeps through the cattle on horseback. The day following Felice's return he used a top buggy behind a massive brown mare named Daisy.

He was gone until dusk. Felice worried, but eventually when he saw the rig coming he stopped worrying.

The next day Travis did the same thing, he used the buggy and returned at dusk. This time he came from an easterly direction and had met no one.

He and Felice cut winter wood the next two days, until Travis said they should quit for awhile.

That night when Felice went outside, a light glowed from the main house. Travis had always been a hard sleeper, but not this particular night. At one time, years back, that had been the reason his wife amusedly chided him: he had gone to sleep on their wedding night.

Felice did the chores. That was his principal obligation. He arose before sun-up to do them. Large animals did not own watches nor know how to use them, they functioned according to stomachs. Felice fed early to avoid being growled at because hungry critters, especially horses, whinnied loudly enough to raise the devil.

This particular morning, an hour or so before *el jefe* appeared there had been no nickering, but in the corral where there should have been three saddle animals, there were four.

The strange animal was as leggy as a thoroughbred. He also had the small ears and the large, intelligent eyes.

Felice fed. Afterwards he walked twice around the strange horse. It could not be bothered, it was trying to devour an entire flake of hay by itself and flattened its ears if other horses came close. Felice found the brand where Mexicans occasionally put one; on the inside of a hind leg. It was one of those curlicued marks typically Mexican. It had curves which *gringo* brands didn't have; they were made with straight lines.

Felice went to his *jacal* to make breakfast and for the eleven thousandth time wished he had a woman; the poorest of them were better cooks than the best of men.

He was at the table eating when he heard the loud squawk.

Travis was by nature an early riser, even when he no longer had to do everything himself, he would awaken in the dark. He might not get dressed in readiness for the new day but ingrained habit ensured he would bed down in the dark and arise in darkness.

This particular morning Travis was returning from his visit to the outhouse, was growling in the direction of the bedroom when he heard what he would have sworn was the muted grumble of a bear.

He stopped dead still to listen. The noise was not repeated. Eventually he faced the closed door beyond which that snarl or whatever it had been, had originated.

Under his breath he said, 'Son of a bitch!' and yanked open the door.

In the darkness there was nothing to discern until after Travis had finished his prowl and even then it wasn't movement but words that yanked the slack out and left him looking in the direction of the bed. A sturdy arm moved phantom-like and a candle brightened things.

Travis said, 'Jesus Christ!'

The man in the bed said, 'I'll shave. You won't notice the sameness.'

Travis approached the bed, the same bed William had slept in since childhood. He looked around for the chair that had worn and soiled clothing draped on it, which he ignored, and sat down. He'd never had rubbery legs before in his life.

The candle was adequate because beyond its reach there was full darkness. Eventually Travis recovered from a variety of shock he had only experienced once or twice in his life. He leaned a little as he said, 'You did it, didn't you?'

'Did what?' the bewhiskered man in the bed said, and added more sarcastically, 'Whatever it was I did it. You haven't changed. Well hell, I didn't expect that you had. Hand me those britches you're settin' on.'

Travis didn't comply, he continued to lean in that tense manner. 'Shot that boy you used to go explorin' with.'

William sat up and held out his hand. Travis gave him the trousers as he arose from the chair. 'Sherman was here lookin' for you.'

William answered as he cinched the pants. 'He's the law now?'

Travis flung over the boots, shirt and hat. 'He's been marshal since after you left . . . William, you can't stay here.'

The taller, bearded man finished dressing and considered his father. 'No, of course I can't, me bein' me an' you bein' you. I wouldn't have come at all except . . . well, I had the urge. For me there's lots of memories. I came with a cattle drive. They don't know I came from here years back. Don't sweat, after I've eaten I'll leave. You got a razor?'

Travis nodded. 'Go out back to the wash rack. I'll bring the razor. How come you to grow whiskers anyway? Your ma didn't like 'em.'

For the younger man the conversation had ended. He brushed past on his way to the place beyond the kitchen which was where he'd cleaned up the long years, when he'd had to stand on a box, until the last day he'd washed out there.

He heard the horses squawking over the last stems of meadow hay, breathed deeply of predawn chill as he'd done as a lad, and shaved. He only heard the horses being cranky until he dried off a face as smooth as a spanked baby's bottom, and another face became visible over his shoulder in the mirror where Felice was standing like stone looking toward the wash rack.

He finished drying off, draped the towel from its peg, turned and raised his voice.

'Hello, Felice. You never change, do you?'

He got no answer as the startled man he had called to disappeared in the wink of an eye.

Back inside where his father was frying meat at the stove William said, 'How old would you say Felice is? He looks exactly the way I last saw him.'

Except for slight noticeable stiffness in his father's back at the stove he got no indication that Travis had heard him.

Not having eaten since early the previous day the younger Culley kept his face lowered and his fork hand busy.

Travis finished first. He rocked back, lifted the coffee cup, looked straight across the table, and spoke as though he hadn't been addressed at the stove.

'What kind of a horse you got? I can loan you one with lots of bottom. You'll have to lead the other one until it's safe to leave him behind. I don't think Sherm'll come snoopin' for maybe a couple of hours.'

William carried his plates to the pan atop the stove, eased them into nearly boiling water and returned to the table and watched his father.

Travis's expression was hard to decipher and he offered no clue until William left the kitchen, was not gone long and seemed uncertain as they faced each other until Travis went to a chair and sat down so his unsteady legs would not give him away. He said, 'You shaved.'

William misinterpreted that statement. 'I left the razor out back beside the basin . . . I'm obliged.'

Travis was having some kind of trouble, he alternately looked at his son and in the direction of the parlour where there were pictures from years back.

William did not extend his hand. 'Which is the horse you'll loan me?'

'Felice'll know. Its name is War Bonnet . . . Better be on your way.'

William left the house, saddle-bags over his shoulder. His father remained seated in the kitchen until he was certain William was gone. Then he went out to the porch, sat and rocked until Felice appeared diffidently and waited for Travis to break the silence which he did.

'Felice, you know where I keep the whiskey in the house. Fetch it for me — please.'

Two things troubled Felice: he was not allowed in the house. He had been in there many years back when Travis's wife had died. The second thing that brought him up short was that 'please'. It wasn't like Travis Culley to say please.

Felice went inside, found the bottle and returned with it. As Travis took it and before he pulled the stopper he said, 'You notice somethin' about the boy?'

Felice fidgeted. 'He come with whiskers an' he don't have them when he leave.'

'No! You damned idiot . . . he looks like his mother!'

3

Old Sandy

True to expectations the cattle, their drovers and two wagons carrying everything from chaps for brush country, whiskey for snake bite and food for the long stretches without town, made camp east of Culleyvile a couple of miles, and the drovers arrived in town to the apprehension of some and enthusiasm of others, particularly the saloonman, the storekeeper, the blacksmith and Emory Hubbard, the only medical man within a week's ride in most directions.

Local stockmen, having been warned in advance, pushed their own cattle as far as they could to avoid an intermingling of brands.

For Travis Culley there was the kind of anxiety that sprang from his son's disappearance as one of the hired drovers, and the strong possibility that they would innocently mention their missing trail companion. Travis told Felice, William had to be a damned fool to hire on with a drive destined to pass anywhere near Culleyville, and Felice developed the habit of watching for riders coming from the direction of Culleyville.

A rider did appear, the same one who had visited before, Culleyville's town marshal.

Travis and Felice were worming some skinny cows in the corral behind the barn when the marshal appeared. Travis left Felice with the cattle and went to the porch with Marshal Kandelin. He had an idea why the lawman had come calling and it was right. They no more than got settled on the porch before the marshal said, 'Travis, the drover crew's in town. Tell me somethin', why didn't Will use another name an' why did he hire on with an outfit coming our way?'

Travis couldn't answer either question so he excused himself, went inside for the bottle and a pair of matching small jolt glasses which provided him with enough time to offer an answer.

Back on the porch he said, 'He likely didn't know they was coming here; this close. About the name, I got no idea, unless he's proud of it.'

Sherm put aside the emptied small glass and gave the older man a long look in silence.

Eventually he said, 'Travis, their range boss knows now who William is and what he did.' It was a statement not a question.

The older man began rocking and gazed straight ahead. 'I got no answers for you, Sherm.'

'Was he here, Travis?'

The older man stopped rocking but did not turn his face. 'I told you I'd do what I could.'

Kandelin abruptly stood up. He and the older man exchanged a look before the lawman said, 'He's been here and

46

left on one of your horses.'

The older man arose with colour coming into his face. 'Sherman, I figured this day would come an' I honestly wish it hadn't.'

Kandelin made a grimacing smile. 'You're not goin' to answer the question, are you, Travis?'

The older man made a death's-head smile. 'You're welcome here any time you're of a mind to come by.'

Travis picked up the small glasses and entered the house. His visitor left the porch, went out to his horse, swung up and was evening up the reins when Felice appeared in the barn's large doorless opening. Felice was expressionless. He and the lawman sat for a moment looking at each other without words passing before Sherm Kandelin straightened up and smiled at Felice. 'I'm goin' to dragoon everyone that's got a horse and comb the territory. We'll find him.'

Felice remained motionless and mute until the mounted man was well away then he went to the house, knocked and when Travis arrived he said, 'I give him a map to the Devil's Den area in the red rocks. He can use one of them caves.'

Travis came out onto the porch and squinted. Kandelin was a moving speck loping in the direction of town. Without taking his eyes off the diminishing lawman, Travis said, 'Damn it to hell, Felice, we're in it. Like it or not we're up to our gizzards in it — on the wrong side.'

Later, Lisbeth Deane rode out on a borrowed big old pudding-footed horse and Travis nodded for Felice to care for the animal. He took the woman to the porch, sat her in the rocker and said, 'Any word from your brother?'

She produced a crumpled piece of paper and handed it to him. He read it twice and handed it back. 'I'm right glad he's feelin' well. I can't get over Will shootin' someone who was his partner when they were growin' up.'

She hadn't spoken, but she spoke

now as she arose and handed him a small weighty bundle. She smiled. 'I've known single men. They don't eat well . . . Mister Culley, neither me nor my brother got hard feelings. You saw in his letter he don't believe Will shot him.'

He accompanied her to the horse, waited until she was in the saddle then smiled. 'I wish you'n William could get together.'

She left the yard in a walk and when Felice appeared, Travis handed him the bundle. 'It's woman cooked. You'n me'll have supper in the house . . . Felice?'

'*Si*, yes, *jefe*.'

'Nothin', let's go open the bundle.'

When Lisbeth got back to town the marshal was waiting. She told him it would be a short while but he was welcome to come inside so they could talk while she cobbled supper together.

He was agreeable, but fate, or destiny, or something anyway intervened.

The head drover, a weathered, thin-lipped individual who was grey at the temples had been told where he might find the local lawman, came to the door, asked Sherm to step outside for a moment and Lisbeth made arrangements to postpone supper until Sherm returned.

It wasn't much of a wait, the head drover knew about young Culley and offered to lie over and help in the manhunt for as long as it took. He told Sherm some years back he had been a lawman down in Texas and felt honour-bound, since he was responsible for bringing an outlaw to the Culleyville area, to help run him down.

Sherm accepted the offer. He had a number of local men who owned horses and were primed and ready to begin the hunt in the morning; the trail boss said he and his riders would meet Sherman and the other possemen at the livery barn.

When he went back inside and saw Lisbeth Deane's expression of enquiry he explained everything to her.

It was later, after supper, that she

told him something he hadn't heard before: she'd had a schoolgirl fondness for Will Culley.

An hour later, Sherman went to his quarters at the Culleyville Hotel, a worked-over, barracks-kind of building built for railroad workers many years earlier. The railroad had never materialized and the building was suitable for what it became, but locals shied from calling it a hotel. They referred to it as a rooming-house which was actually what it had become.

In the morning, he appeared at the livery barn more than an hour before stragglers began arriving, mostly loaded for bear with rifles, carbines, ammunition and fresh horses.

The trail boss, a grizzled, weathered man called Curly Smith because he had no hair under the hat on the top of his head, roughly introduced his three trail drovers, counting himself, and not only had a booted Winchester saddle gun, but a Colt around his middle with an under-and-over large

51

calibre derringer inside his shirt.

His only worry was that when his camp was left unprotected thieves from town might ride out there, help themselves and stampede the cattle.

Two townsmen volunteered to go out there and mind things until the posse riders returned. From the trail boss's expression it was clear he welcomed those volunteers with a whole heart.

Lisbeth Deane watched the riders leave town heading southward. She was seen at the window and received hand waves in the chilly poor light.

Before bedding down the previous night, Sherman had worked out a way to best conduct his manhunt. For one thing he hadn't been totally surprised during his last meeting with Travis Culley that the cowman wasn't as totally set against his son as he had claimed to be only a few days earlier.

On the basis of that hunch he conferred with the trail boss until an agreement was reached to comb the

Culley range first.

Sherman knew the territory, he had explored much of it. They went westerly on a tangent that kept them well in the northern part of the Culley range, spread out with several townsmen at a distance from one another in a ragged line always within sight.

Sherman and the trail boss maintained a shouting closeness.

One of the drovers flushed a band of coyotes. The animals raced like the wind. One rider rode in pursuit until the trail boss signalled for him to come back.

The sun eventually brought warmth. With excellent visibility and new-day heat, the wide sweep they made pretty well limited anything with two legs or four escaping detection. They were given a wide berth by cattle and as the sun climbed they found horse tracks. Unshod tracks. Once or twice riders would follow the tracks but when they veered in singles or pairs the tracks were abandoned.

With the sun almost directly over-head, Sherman came to a willow creek where the horses were watered and rested. It was at this place with willows on both banks that a townsman approached Sherm and pointed in the direction of a landswell that rose gradually toward a mesa with trees atop it.

The man didn't say anything, just pointed with an upraised arm.

There was a horseman atop a distant ridge, clearly watching the riders. Smith, the trail boss, squinted, but the horseman was too distant. Smith shielded his eyes as he said, 'Takes a man back. That's how the Comanche spied on folks. Set up there like a statue an' when they raised an arm there'd be the rest of 'em come up from the far side hollerin' and comin' like the wind.'

Several other men joined the group around the marshal and trail boss. An older man said, 'It ain't no Inian. He's ridin' a white man's saddle.'

Smith made a dry remark. 'You got

54

better eyesight than I have. Is he a white man?'

The townsman answered minimally. 'Can't tell from here, but maybe.'

Sherm bridled his animal, snugged up the cinch and swung astride. He led off in the direction of the distant watcher.

For as long as was required for the posse riders to reach the country that began to slope, the watcher remained up there on his mount. When the possemen began the ascent he turned without haste and disappeared down the far side.

That townsman who had mentioned Indians scouting in this fashion watched the horseman pass from sight and shook his head. He as well as the others knew there had been no Indians in this territory for years, but that townsman couldn't have been convinced of that as he and his companions continued their ascent.

Sherm picked up the tracks where the watcher had been. He was atop the ridge leaning sideways studying horse sign when Curly Smith, the trail boss, came up, drew rein and spoke while peering ahead where there was no sign of the watcher. He said, 'Disappeared like a digger squirrel.'

It was true; except for the jumble of huge reddish rocks the far-side country was empty. There was not even the customary bunch of Culley cattle.

Sherm gestured with an upraised arm for the riders to fan out again. He and the trail boss remained together.

The sun was up there with its increasing heat.

One of the drovers abruptly hooked his mount into a lope. Within moments the others closed up a little, trying to locate whatever had spooked the drover.

They were still east of the red rocks, cautiously studying the countryside around them, when that trail man up ahead closer to the mammoth boulders, let go with a whoop that could be heard for some distance and followed his shout with a gunshot.

Sherm and Curly Smith boosted their mounts into a run. They were east of the red rocks, the other possemen more cautiously slow, loping behind them.

Sunlight reflected off pistols in upraised hands.

Sherman and the trail boss reached the big rocks together. Able to see westward on the far side of the rocks, two hard-riding horsemen were widening the distance with every jump. One of them threw a wild shot back. The possemen scattered despite there being very little danger.

Curly Smith raised his right arm, the signal to stop. His men eased off, reined in his direction and halted close to the trail boss. Several men favoured continuing the pursuit.

Curly Smith dismounted, watched the fleeing riders grow smaller and said nothing until the distance between those being chased and those doing the chasing was too great, even for rifles.

Sherman halted, looked around and said, 'All right. We know where to pick up the sign.'

A young townsman holding his carbine aloft said, 'We can't catch 'em.' The escaping riders were ant-size in the westerly distance.

There was shade among the huge red rocks and it was welcome. The horses needed it more than the men, but they, too, were willing to rest.

A trail drover went looking for the shadiest place, found it and sank to the ground as he made an announcement. 'I know who that tallest one was. I was ridin' with him to the punch bowl country where we got hired on for this drive. His name's Will Culley. We met up in the Comanche part of Texas. That's him.'

Curly Smith spoke disgustedly. 'Will Culley. That's how I hired him on. Marshal?'

Sherman responded. 'Will Culley.'

'You sure it's the same man?'

'No, I'm not sure, but why did he run

58

from us? I never got a good look but puttin' it together . . . '

Heat reflected off the red rocks. After a long pow-wow it was decided to go back, and on the return ride when Sherman pointed out some distant log structures and said that was the home of the fugitive it was suggested that they ride over there.

Sherm didn't object, but he warned his companions about Travis Culley's disposition.

No one seemed intimidated so Sherman altered course with the heat more objectionable than it had been back in the red-rock country.

Questions were asked and answered until the possemen knew all they had to know about the fugitive's father, by which time they were close enough to make out peckerwood holes in the logs and to see the man on the porch of his house with the saddle gun in his hands.

Sherman's last words were given in a softened voice. 'No matter what, don't anyone lower a hand off the swells of your saddles.'

Travis'd had time to make his judgement of the riders and the lead rider leading them. He did not have to ask questions, he had seen posses before, quite a few times. When Sherm and the rugged man beside him drew rein, the marshal spoke before anyone else could.

'Travis,' he said, and nodded. The older man neither responded nor nodded his head.

Sherman cleared his throat. 'We're lookin' for William.'

'I figured you would be. He's not here, Sherm. I told you . . . he's not welcome here an' he knows it. What right you got leadin' them fellers over private land? You got half an hour to get off my range.'

Curly Smith, the former lawman, made a mistake when he said, 'Mister, it's in the law that outlaws can be chased wherever it takes to run 'em down.'

Travis's gaze went to the trail boss. 'Is

60

that a fact? Mister, you're where you got no right to be an' I'm bein' right decent givin' all of you half an hour to be off it. An' don't come back.'

That townsman who had first seen the watcher back yonder, and who had no particular liking for Travis, looked him squarely in the face and spoke without raising his voice. 'Mister Culley, before we leave I'd take it kindly if you'd answer one question for me.'

'I don't have to talk to you at all, Sandy. How come you to take up with this trash? What is the question?'

'I've known your hired man for ten years. Was that him we saw earlier ridin' with another feller out near them red rocks? Was that Felice?'

Travis's grip on the carbine tightened until the knuckles were white. He returned the other man's stare without blinking, or for a while, saying a word.

He returned his attention to the town marshal. 'Sherm! Get em the hell off my land! I mean it! *Right gawddamn now!*'

Travis's saddle gun came up off the porch floor to be gripped in both hands. For seconds there was no movement nor sound, not until Sherman Kandelin reined around and led off past the barn, through the gate at the far end and beyond where he broke over into a lope and held to it even when he twisted to look back. Travis was still on the porch with his saddle gun. He looked child-size.

Curly Smith eased up to ride stirrup with the marshal. As they loped together, Smith said, 'You was right. He's a mean old son of a bitch. I've seen 'em like him before. But he wouldn't have used that Winchester.'

Sherman twisted to look back where the old man was standing exactly as they'd left him, holding that Winchester in both hands. He straightened back around and without saying a word he showed a wintery smile to the trail boss.

When they got back to town and left their animals to be cared for by the liveryman, Curly Smith and his riders headed for the eatery. Sherm caught one posseman by the arm to detain him at the jailhouse. He offered a plug which the other man declined as he sat in a chair gazing at the marshal.

Sherm said, 'You liked to've got someone hurt out there, Sandy.'

The tall, lean, older man was Sanford Lamont, Culleyville's saddle and harness-maker, a quiet artisan, locally known as a very direct individual.

'He wouldn't have brought it off, Sherm. Up where you an' the trail boss was settin' you was ahead an' to my left.'

Sherm sank down at his desk. 'And . . . ?'

'Had it in my hand aimed straight at his chest. Like this.'

The harness-maker seemed to barely shift in the chair, just enough for Sherm to see the large work-roughened hand closed around a big-bore nickel-plated derringer.

Sandy returned the belly gun to his

pocket, arose and smiled. 'You didn't recognize that watcher; I did. It was the old man's dog robber. Overweight Felice Obregon. An' the horse he was ridin' was a line-back buckskin the old man likes better'n others. He's gettin' old; he's sheddin' his grinders. The old man paid me three dollars to make a special headstall for Travis's Mex bit . . . '

Sherm leaned back off the desk. 'You knew 'em from that distance?'

Sandy, about as old as Travis, broadly smiled. 'Sonny, there's lots of things about me that don't work any more but in my line of work a man's got to coddle his hands an' his eyes.' As the harness-maker went to the door, still smiling, he also said, 'Travis's Messican's been puttin' on weight. It was him up there on that buckskin horse. I know'm both.'

Sherman stood up. 'Sandy, you up to your neck in work?'

The saddle-maker's smile remained fixed in place. 'Hardly workin'. Why?'

'You know that red-rock country?'

'Like the back of my hand. Thirty years back I took up a hundred an' sixty acres of railroad land.' The harness-maker hesitated, walked back to the chair, sat down, pushed out a pair of long legs and let his smile fade a tad. 'I think I might be ahead of you, Sherm. I know the country. What about it?'

Sherm sat back down. 'You'd know that country better'n I would?'

'Most likely.'

'On the ride back I got to thinkin' what you said awhile back . . . '

'He was watchin' for us, Marshal. Most likely saw us leave town and got out there first. You tell me if I'm wrong. You think the Messican was set to warn we was comin'?'

Sherm grinned. 'Sly old bastard. Felice spied on us and warned some-one.'

'That'd be Travis's boy, sonny; an' you figure me knowin' the territory, Will's hid out somewhere?'

'Could you maybe find him, Sandy?'

'Well now, sonny, me'n an old mangy cat I found got to eat. He come to my back-alley door about a year back. I feed him an' he listens. I call him Gen'ral Grant . . . he don't eat as much as I do.'

'Two bits a day, Sandy.'

'I got no horse, Marshal.'

'Two bits a day an' a horse.'

'When do you want to go back out there?'

'Tomorrow at sun-up.'

For the second time the lanky older man stood up. 'I'll be down at the barn waitin', Marshal.'

4

The Red-Rock Country

The horses were saddled. Sandy and the liveryman were seeing who could out-lie the other one. When the marshal arrived, Sandy would not budge until all three of them had a cup of the liveryman's coffee, which had been brewed in hell for imps.

The harness-maker hadn't been on a horse much in thirty years but some things once learned are not forgotten. His problem was the buffalo rifle. It wouldn't fit a normal saddle boot. And the large, old, long-barrelled pistol in its ancient hip holster, gouged. But Sandy had eaten and was now embarking on what he was convinced would be his last great adventure.

He talked, recalled other times when he'd ridden out — for bloody-hand

Indians in those days. The more he reminisced the more Sherman speculated on how much was the truth and how much was not.

When old Sandy recalled his escape from the Custer fight in '76 the onliest whiteskin to get away with his hair, Sherm decided that over the years fact and fantasy had gotten so intermingled that Sandy was no longer able to separate one from the other.

It was still dark — and cold — when they distantly made out the monument-sized jumble of red rocks and from there on Sandy and the past coincided. The past became yesterday, particularly in Travis Culley's yard in front of the log house.

He ended that recollection with a single statement. 'I would have blown his damned head off before he could have got that carbine halfway up.'

The ensuing silence presented Sherm Kandelin with an opportunity to mention Travis's son.

Sandy was prepared. 'I've known him

since he'd come to town with his folks in the supply wagon. He'd come to the shop, wanted to learn things. Marshal, sometimes they grow up tamed an' that's not right. They'd ought to be allowed to run a little wild. Tell me, just why does the law want him?'

'For stoppin' a stage with two other fellers an' shootin' the whip.'

'Killed him, did he?'

'No. From what I've heard he hit him in the upper leg.'

Sandy snorted. 'I set with that boy in the alley teachin' him how to aim. When to take 'em out an' when to send 'em home cryin'.'

Sherman raised his right arm. 'A few years back I explored those rocks. Some as big as a ship. They got caves an' tunnels.'

'You think he's holed up in there?'

'I think it's possible, an' if that's so Felice would be bringin' supplies.'

The marshal rode in silence studying the acreage of red rocks.

The last time he'd been out here he'd

sat in shade wondering how the immense boulders had got where they were, and how they had come to have their colour. To his knowledge there were no other rocks of that colour.

He made the mistake of mentioning this. His companion launched into an explanation: the Indians had brought them to where they stood now back when Indians had been ten feet tall and correspondingly muscled up.

Sherm drew rein about a half-mile out, sat watching a new-day sun work its special magic. Sandy interrupted his ponderings.

'I'll tell you, sonny, they come in the night and put the red colouring all over them. Even on the inside. About this time in the morning, they sweep it all up, put it in the biggest *parfleche* pouch you ever saw, climb up into the heavens and float up north to Canada where they put them pouches in a special place, eat an' sleep until it is time to come back and make them red again.'

Sherman led his horse until he found

a place it could crop some graze and left it there, hobbled. Sandy's livery animal was treated the same way. It was a gelding and a hay eater. Fresh grass flavoured with dew . . . put its head down and never raised it.

The harness-maker raised his face and slowly turned it from side to side. When he saw that he was being watched he seemed slightly embarrassed. 'Scent first,' he said. 'Sometimes they'll be cookin' breakfast.'

Sherm stood in the poor light. The rocks were huge with a tapering off. He walked without haste and eventually sat down on a boulder. He had been looking for a path. It was still too dark. When he arose to stand, looking up, he grunted and led off again. This time without looking down.

When they were among the rocks, old Sandy quartered like a hunting dog. Where he eventually halted, Sherman followed the old man's line of sight. There were no tracks but on the hind side of a massively immense rock he pointed to a place where moccasined feet had left their sign over the centuries.

Sherm had misgivings, but he followed Sandy using faint gouges which were barely adequate for finger and toe holds.

Sandy for all his age and housebound infirmities used those markers with the enthusiasm of a monkey.

Part-way up, the world brightened in a wide line. Increased visibility helped but not much and once when the marshal looked down his impression was that of someone clinging on a steamboat-sized red rock in the middle of eternity. Faint daylight shone against the front, behind where the climbers were; he took down a shallow breath, resumed climbing and did not look down again.

The last yard or so the gouges were easier to climb but more hair-raising.

Ahead, Sandy made a lunge and stood upright. He had reached the top-out and although visibility was still limited, scenting wasn't.

As Sherman toed into the last moccasin track the old man stooped with an extended hand. He grunted with the effort while leaning back until the lawman was safely in place. He released his handhold and softly said, 'Cookin'. You smell it?'

Sherm smelled nothing. He leaned to peer back down where he had climbed and shook his head. 'Just how in hell do we get back down from here?' he asked.

Sandy scowled. 'Same way we clumb up. You lie flat an' sort of press flat an' slither.'

Sandy's concern was elsewhere. 'Turn, sonny. All the way around an' back. Slow. Like this. Now then, did you catch it?'

Sherman nodded. 'Wood smoke.'

'Where's it comin' from?'

The marshal raised an arm. 'Northerly somewhere.'

Sandy went to the rim above the ancient marks, peered down, turned and said, 'Remember now: sort of spreadeagle against the rock. Feel with your toes for them gouged-out places. Watch the way I do it.'

Sherm watched and marvelled. Sandy Lamont had to be at least seventy, more likely in his eighties, and he went back down with both arms spread wide, his body pressed hard against red rock.

Daylight arrived over the top of the tall sentinel where Sherm stood breathing deeply. He got down on all fours, let his legs dangle until he found a gouge and descended.

Sandy was waiting down where nothing had improved, neither the visibility nor the temperature. Chilly as it was, Sherman was sweating like a stud wood tick.

Sandy didn't hesitate, he began picking his way. The wood-fire scent was only occasionally noticeable at ground level, but the old man kept going and did not stop until they had come out atop a flat ledge. To reach this place he had been gradually climbing.

In prehistoric times there had been a ravine. Over the millennia windblown dirt had filled the ravine in until the rocks on both sides were an equal height.

Sandy dropped flat, gestured for his companion to do the same and got as comfortable as it was possible to get belly-down on cold rock.

When the lawman was within six or maybe eight feet of the abrupt northerly drop off, Sandy crawled over and made noises like their existence depended on being quiet.

He said, 'If they got a camp it'll likely be there,' and wrinkled his nose.

Sherman had the scent but it seemed faint. When he raised up like a lizard, the wood-fire scent was stronger.

Sandy crawled away to the lawman's left and pressed until he became part of the red stone world. Sherman, out of his element, alternately watched the old man and the wide, grassy place below. Although he tried hard he could find nothing that could be a lean-to or even a brush shelter. Sandy made gestures for the town marshal to be patient and rolled up on to one side to indicate what he meant.

The chill gradually abated. Sherman noticed it less as daylight improved and from his abrupt promontory, with the sun brightening the reddish shades of the great rocks opposite his place of vantage.

Both men caught wisps of wood-smoke scent but neither could discern the source of either the fire or its smell. Not until daylight had advanced over and above most of the rocks was it even possible to see the opposite stone face above and behind the small meadow.

The old man rolled close and raised a rigid arm without speaking. A horse-man had entered the meadow from the west. Sandy sounded elated when he said, 'Obregon. You see him? That's Travis's Messican.'

The marshal remained quiet until the horseman was part-way toward the meadow and the rider stood in his stirrups and made a short, keening whistle, sat back down and reined to a halt.

The rider looked southward, along the abrupt side of the place where the two stalkers could not be seen, unless they moved which neither of them did.

Eventually the rider dismounted and led his horse further toward the meadow. To Sherman he seemed uneasy or impatient, especially when he raised his hand to make another of those keening whistles. He had his hand still in place when he froze. The second man was afoot. He was taller, not as heavy and appeared less anxious. Sherman looked past for the place the second man had come from.

Sandy nudged him and shook his head. 'Never mind,' he softly said, 'stay with me now.'

The older man began inching backward until they were both safe from detection, then the harness-maker stood up, jerked his head and led off back the way they had come, until they were clear of the filled-in arroyo, then he changed course and almost trotted.

He stopped only once, when the trail they were using abruptly divided, one spur going south, the other spur curling around northward. The old man didn't hesitate, he took the northward path and did not slacken his gait although the new path had dozens of rocks which had tumbled from higher up. The sun would not reach down this far until it was directly overhead, which made Sherman irritable after he stumbled several times.

The harness-maker made another twist and this time he was on a path that had very few boulders in it. He stopped, leaned briefly, straightened up and beckoned for the marshal to hasten forward.

When they were together the old man didn't have to say why he had to abruptly stop. There were shod-horse tracks underfoot. Sandy pointed in the opposite direction. Sherm went back about a yard tracing out the sign. Sandy hissed and signalled for him to come back. The old man led off again and only intermittently paused to reaffirm he was following those shod-horse imprints.

The last time he halted, Sherman could look eastward and see the full distance of that meadow he had seen from up above. He leaned in the shadow of a pinnacle looking for the horse and two men. They were nowhere in sight.

Sandy came over near to smiling. 'Now you know who's in there an' why he come.'

Sherman said, 'Where did the tall man go?'

The answer wasn't what he expected. 'You stay with this rock standin' straight up. I'll be across the way. When he comes back we got him.'

'Hell, maybe he won't come back. Maybe there's another way out.'

'There's only the way he come, sonny. Dead ahead easterly there's big rocks one after another. I can use some rest. If he don't come back right away . . . keep listenin', Marshal. He's ridin' a shod horse. In rock country like this he's goin' to bump 'em.'

Sherman got behind the pinnacle to watch the older man disappear on the opposite side of the meadow's mouth where there was no plinth but horse-size boulders were abundant.

Sherman sat on the ground, reconciled to a long wait. His plinth stood as straight as a tree for about fifty, sixty feet. From the appearance of its top, whatever had broken it at that height had to have been another rock of considerable weight and impetus.

He thought about his companion, old or not, slipping, sliding and jumping over rocks at a hurrying gait was something not many younger men could have accomplished. Old Sandy seemed to be in his element. Sherman speculated. Satisfied the rider they were going to ambush was, as Sandy had said, Felice, Culley's Mexican, why was he in here and if Travis had perhaps sent him, why then, Travis's convincing snarl that he wanted nothing to do with his son was not true.

It was hard not to doze. Hours in the cold predawn followed by climbing huge rocks with the sun finally hitting him hard, made him understandably drowsy.

So drowsy he was fast asleep when a snarling voice not only awakened him, but startled him so badly he went for his holstered Colt and dropped it.

The man on the horse had both hands as high as his shoulders, reins dangling from the left hand. He seemed to Sherm to be unable to move or speak.

Sandy's old horse pistol would intimidate anyone. He hadn't cocked it, but it was tilted with perfect aim at the horseman as Sandy, using the same snarling tone that had awakened the marshal, spoke again.

'Where's them saddle-bags you had when you rode in here? Get off that horse, you pot-bellied bastard. Where's

Will Culley holed up? You lie to me an' I'll blow your head off. *Where is he?*'

Felice came down from the saddle on the opposite side. Sherman waited for him to go for his sidearm which Sandy could not see from the horse's other side.

Sherman lifted out his six-gun and waited. Felice made no move toward his holster. Sandy leaned across the empty saddle with his old hawgleg pistol no more than ten-twelve inches from the Mexican's face.

Felice bleated, 'Don't shoot. I go just riding.'

Sandy gestured with his gun for Felice to go to the head of his horse, which the Mexican did and Sandy showed a death's-head grin and lowered the old six-gun until it was bearing on Felice's middle when Sandy said, '*Where is he?*'

Sherman moved clear of his plinth and something happened no one expected. The voice unmistakably belonged to Travis Culley. It came from somewhere behind the lawman. It sounded unpleasant when it told the harness-maker to drop his gun.

Sandy hung fire. He twisted slightly to find the man who had spoken. Sherman spoke next, 'Sandy, holster it.'

The older man answered curtly. 'He's not goin' to shoot me, Sherman, because if he does I'll kill this son of a bitch.'

Sherman tried again. 'Sandy, he's behind me. You're goin' to get us both shot. Put up the damned hawgleg!'

The leather-man's reply was forcefully given. 'Marshal, I never turned chicken in my life.' There was a long pause, then more. 'Travis? Is that you? Go ahead, pull the trigger. I'll take this possum-bellied son of a bitch with me. Travis, spit or close the window!'

Marshal Kandelin tried one more time. 'Sandy! Put the hawgleg back where it belongs. It's not worth gettin' shot over.'

Before the harness-maker could speak, the person none of them could see beat him to it. 'Sandy, you damned old idiot. No one's callin' you. It's not a fight. I'll tell you why he's up here. Put up that gun. Hell, that old gun went out of style thirty years ago. *Put it up!*'

The old gun did not waver but the man who had it pushing in his stomach moved, he shook like a dog coming out of water when he said, 'Nobody's to get hurt, Mister Saddle-maker. I was just doin' an errand. You can't kill people for doin' errands.'

Sandy let the gun sag but he did not holster it until Travis came from behind two large boulders. His six-gun was in its holster. He was thoroughly disgusted. He walked up to the other old man, knocked the hawgleg aside and said, 'He was takin' supplies to William.' Travis turned on the lawman. 'What in hell . . . Sherm, do you know this is my deeded land, where you're standin' and for one hell of a distance in every other direction. You got a right to be here? Show me the paper says you got the right, or go back where you'n him hobbled your animals, get astride an' don't even look back.'

Sandy braced Travis. 'Or what? You goin' to get the law after us? You blind old bastard, *he is the law!*'

Sherman gave up. He walked over to the others and faced Travis. 'There's a warrant out for Will. If he's holed up in these rocks you take me to him.'

Travis eyed the marshal through an interval of silence, then said, 'You show me proof William shot young Burton an' you can have him. You got it, Sherm?'

'I don't have it, an' the best I can do is telegraph Deming for it.'

'An' meanwhile William can go free? I'll guarantee he'll be around if you come for him. Sherm, is that fair or not?'

It was fair. Sherm inclined his head and Travis faced his Mexican. 'Get on home. There's some wormy cows I put in the corral. Dose hell out of 'em an' turn 'em loose.'

Sandy growled at Travis, 'You'd let

'em take your boy? Let me tell you somethin': I never liked you but handin' over your own kin . . . Marshal? I know just about every livable place in these damned rocks, if you're ready.'

Sherm considered Travis. He hadn't been the same since the death of his wife. His son and the marshal had been friends years back. He remembered things the son had said about his father. Despite those things, Travis had sent supplies to his son and had come too, when his son'd had to run for it and there was something the harness-maker had said, it really wasn't right a father handing over his son, law or no law. He had a moment of seeing himself as others might see him and didn't like it.

He faced Travis. 'You know where Will is holed up? It don't much matter, but I'd like to talk to him.'

Travis's eyes narrowed. 'I know where he is. How bad do you want to lock him in your jail?'

'Not very bad,' the marshal stated.

'You'n . . . him . . . go get your

animals. I'll be here when you get back. Sandy . . . ? All right, I'm into it up to my ears but I'll be here when Sherm gets back. You can go on back to town.'

Sandy shrugged, looked at the marshal who nodded, then began walking toward where they had left their animals with Sherm following close behind.

Travis went to the place he'd left his mount, made it more comfortable to get through the long wait and told the horse he'd never liked that damned saddle-maker.

The sun was high. Travis sat in red-rock shade. Ever since he could remember this had been a haunted place. The Indians had still been around when Travis and his wife had taken up land. He had gotten along with them very well. They had gone with him on horse-back exploring the red-rock area. That far back their platforms of the dead had still been in sight. In fact he had cut poles and hauled them up in here for the

Indians. Burial poles.

They had told him of the purity of the red-rock field. It didn't work except for some but it worked. There were only two places such red rocks existed. The land he owned was where one was located.

He sat in shade. It would take some time. He had seen their horses on his way up here. He had plenty of time. The Indians had showed him how a man talked to the spirits. He felt a little silly, but no one could see, so he went through the preparatory symbols and he loudly spoke. There were echoes.

It got hot down in the depths of the rocks. He found a shady place close enough to see the marshal and his companion when they returned.

There wasn't a sound nor a wisp of moving air, just the ancient stillness and warmth. He leaned back against a half-dead old tree.

. . . He was taking a bath. The pool wasn't very big and a large grey bird was watching him. He sank and came up. The bird had waited. He got out of the water and sat on a rock looking at the bird. For awhile neither of them moved, until the bird opened its wings; they made great covering as the bird arose soundlessly. It came straight toward him. When it was above him on its way it shut out the sun. A moment later it was gone, climbing higher until he could not find it against the highest red rocks.

For those few seconds, the shade of its wings had covered him completely.

5

Getting Close

It took a little while before Travis saw the face, but the voice was familiar. 'Hello, Pa.'

'Hello, Son. They're lookin' for you.'

'I know. I saw 'em catch Felice. Durin' the scuffle I ducked back. Mind if I set here?'

'Don't mind at all. There's plenty of shade. Ask you a question, Will; years back I explored these rocks; which cave is yours?'

'You know the one halfway up facin' east? There's sign someone used it long ago.'

Travis nodded. 'Got a rock circle in front?'

'That's it. Thanks for sendin' the grub.'

Travis picked up a twig that had no

bark around it. He slowly etched a map when he said, 'That's the path to the cave?'

His son nodded without speaking. They sat in shade until the older man cocked his head. His son said, 'It'll be Sherm.'

'I expect so. Boy, you goin' back with him?'

'That's what I been ponderin'. I guess I will, but I want to tell you somethin': it wasn't me that shot Al. I didn't shoot at anyone. I saw him go down writhin' like a snake. I was busy tryin' to get away.'

Travis looked around. 'Then who did shoot him?'

'I got no idea. Me'n Tex was makin' a break for it.'

'Who was Tex?'

'Tex Taylor, a feller I met in Deming. He knew when the stages came'n went. He got his ankle caught in some rocks. They thought he was wounded. By the time he could free it the gun guard was standin' over him.'

The oncoming horseman rattled small rocks. When he came into sight Travis and his son were waiting. Before Sherm got close, Travis told his son he'd raise heaven and hell to get Will loose.

Sherm was leading a saddled animal. As he was dismounting, he said, 'Travis, your Messican got the whey scairt out of him.'

Sherm nodded at Will and handed him the reins to the extra horse. As they regarded each other Sherm said, 'You ready, Will?'

'Yeah, I'll go back with you.'

Sherm faced the older man. 'Travis, did you ever shoot a man in the back?'

Will's father showed a bitter small smile as he replied. 'Never did, but there's always a first time.' Travis faced his son. 'Get astride, before you two get to town it'll be dark.'

Will mounted the led horse, fumbled with the reins until he had them evened up then looked down at his father. Travis said, 'Move out. Sherm, I'll come to town tomorrow.'

He stood like one of the plinths watching the pair of younger men head back in the direction of open country.

Will broke the silence that had settled between the marshal and himself when they were clear of the red rocks. 'I never knew my pa real well. I guess he'll stand by me.'

Will was silent for a fair distance then he also said, 'I did some ponderin' back up there. Some fathers seems to me don't feel much for sons until the sons grow up to manhood, then it sort of comes to 'em all at once. Sherm, when you talk to Deming ask them if my gun had been shot when they caught me in that arroyo.'

Sherm softly scowled. 'You didn't shoot Lisbeth's brother?'

'I didn't shoot anyone; I was tryin' to get free of some rocks.'

Sherm was quiet until they were on the outskirts of town by which time it was darker than the inside of a boot, then all he said was, 'Who did shoot him?'

'Damned if I know. Is it too late for us to get somethin' to eat?'

That question did not require an answer. Culleyville's eatery was dark as were most other business establishments. The saloon was lighted. Sherm took his prisoner to the middle of town where his jailhouse was located and locked him in his only strap-steel cell, which resembled a large cage, and went looking for some place he could buy food. The general store had a feeble light showing so Sherm went over there. He had to use a fist on the door before he got a response, then it was not Frank Christy, the owner, it was his daughter Pansy, who outweighed her father. She was smiling when she unlocked the roadway door, but hefty Pansy smiled more than she did anything else. She blocked the doorway until the marshal explained what he wanted and why he wanted it.

Pansy's father, a large, pale-eyed man

had started his general store from scratch and because he liked people he enjoyed serving them, but he loathed bookkeeping, anything that had to do with numbers, so he left the arithmetic to his daughter who was not only good with numbers but enjoyed working with them. As she got the items Sherm wanted and placed them on the counter, she asked questions and he answered them. She loaned him a basket for his purchases, saw him to the door and said. 'I never believed it. I've known Will Culley since our school-days; he wouldn't shoot anyone.'

When Sherm told Will that as they ate in the cell Will smiled. 'Before she got to weighin' more'n I did, I walked her home'n all. We was best friends.'

They exhausted the story of Pansy Christy as they emptied tins of syrupy peaches, some kind of German bread a man could roll from one end of town to the other end without cracking it and talked until daylight about the stage robbery, Will's companions in that enterprise, and Will's father.

The last topic concerned Travis's stirrups. They were made of iron and encased in carved leather and weighed a ton. Travis had found them; his son had no idea where they had been found. He remembered a particular discussion he'd had with his father about anyone using iron stirrups and shook his head. That discussion had ended up in an argument.

After Sherm left the jailhouse to hike up to his room at the rooming-house, Will bedded down on a croaker-sack mattress stuffed with straw. Sherm and the man who had returned to town with him as his prisoner both slept like the dead. Sherm did not awaken until the grumpy individual who owned his made-over 'hotel' came to rattle the door. He was worried; this particular tenant had never before slept after sunrise.

Lisbeth Deane was at the jailhouse waiting when the marshal crossed over from a late breakfast. She knew the man who had shot her brother was locked up. How she knew Sherm didn't ask and she didn't say, but it wasn't much of a mystery; the old gaffer who owned the livery barn rarely failed to pass along any scrap of information the saloonman wouldn't pay for with free jolts of Hiram Walker's inebriating fairy pee.

It was customary for lawmen to sit close by when prisoners had visitors. That's how Sherm heard for the second time that Will denied shooting her brother.

Lisbeth stirred Sherm into action when she told Will she had three dollars saved which she would use now telegraphing down to Deming for the details of Al Burton's getting shot and the part in this affair her brother had been told Will had been involved in.

Sherm told Lisbeth he would have to lock her in the cell with Will, to which she made no objection, and to make double certain there would be no empty cell when he returned he also locked the roadway entrance to his jailhouse, then briskly went up to the telegrapher's cubby hole, wrote out what he wanted sent to the authorities down at Deming and lingered long enough to hear the clicks and clacks of the message being sent.

The telegrapher, a taciturn individual addicted to green eyeshades, asked if there was anything else the town marshal wanted and Sherm, acting mildly embarrassed, left the building, returned to the jailhouse, unlocked the doors and had a peculiar feeling in the centre of his chest as he held the roadway door for Lisbeth's departure and she stood on her toes and kissed Sherm on the cheek before she departed.

Travis Culley appeared in town astride a handsome line-back gelding, which otherwise lacked the markings of a genuine buckskin, before noon. He too had a telegraph message to send and if he hadn't told Sherm about the message summoning a fee lawyer from up north, Sherm might not have known to what extent the father expected to go to save the son from being extradited.

One more time Will had a visitor in his cage. This time the older man promised to fetch eats before his visit was concluded.

As before, Sherm was party to a discussion concerning his prisoner and as with the other time, he kept the discussion going by interposing an occasional remark about his objective to which Will Culley had no objection; in fact, after his father departed young Culley's spirits remained high.

Over a shared supper, Sherm told his prisoner that he had never before seen old Travis Culley in such good spirits. He had even smiled a few times. Will had agreed between mouthfuls; his father was not ordinarily a pleasant person to be around.

The fee lawyer from up north did not arrive in Culleyville for almost ten days, someone else arrived in half that length of time. His name was Arthur Holding, he was one of the highwaymen who had robbed the stage down south when Lisbeth's brother had been shot. He was using the name of Arthur Garfield which happened to be the name of a politician back East by the same name whose ultimate political success was to achieve the US presidency and be assassinated.

He had been in town several days before Hiram Boyard, the saloonman, provided him with the information the stranger sought.

It made it easier to learn that the man he was looking for was in the local jailhouse. The saloonman did not know on what charges the town marshal was holding Culley, but he explained something else that seemed to interest the stranger, not only was the town named after a local individual but that Will Culley's father, for whom the town had been named, was a local rancher presumably with enough wealth to buy and sell most folks many times over.

Holding's reason for being in Culleyville, according to the saloonman, was that of a cattle buyer and having ridden over much of the territory he was convinced the quality of local cattle would make it worth his time to stay awhile and see if he couldn't put together a big enough band of beef to hire riders for a drive to the nearest railroad siding with chutes for the loading of cattle.

The saloonman was ordinarily a purveyor of gossip, it helped when a body was in the saloon business. Of a certainty this story deserved retelling because it quite possibly had the means for making money for local folks.

Old Travis was bringing in a sore-footed bull when he and Felice saw the approaching horseman who appeared heading in their direction.

When the stranger passed through the gate north of the barn, Travis left Felice with the tender-footed bull and went to intercept the stranger.

They met at the tie rack in front of

the house where introductions were exchanged and the visitor thanked Travis in advance before Travis had finished shedding his spurs.

When Travis returned with the little glasses and the bottle his guest was contentedly rocking. He accepted the glass without arising to get it.

Travis said, 'You're a cattle buyer?'

The taller and younger man nodded, saluted with the unraised little glass and downed its content.

Travis perched on the porch railing. 'It's not a good time; fall is better. I don't know as I'll have much to sell this year.'

His visitor seemed settled and comfortable when he said, 'I'll be back. You usually make a drive?'

Travis nodded, retrieved the empty glass and stood up. 'Four, five of us road brand, gather and strike out.' Travis went inside with the glasses and the bottle. When he returned, his visitor was standing, considering as much of the countryside as he could see from the porch. In the distance, the field of red rocks showed massively in the daylight. He was impressed. 'Don't know as I've ever seen a field of rocks that colour.'

The old man gazed in the same direction. 'Lots of In'ian legends.' He made a slight smile. 'Seems like wherever somethin' is unusual gets all sorts of stories about 'em.'

The stranger shoved out his hand and genuinely smiled. 'Much obliged for your hospitality,' he said. 'And the whiskey. Good quality. Maybe I'll come back when it's time for drivin' cattle.'

Travis walked to the dozing horse. They nodded again and when his visitor reined around to head back he was passing beyond sight where the barn hindered visibility when he raised his hand in a casual salute.

In town, either the liveryman or the saloonman were ordinarily good sources of local problems or information. When Sherm went down to lead his horse over to the smithy, the liveryman was waiting. 'He's lookin' for somethin',' the liveryman told the town marshal speaking of the newcomer.

At the jailhouse, Sherm took his prisoner to the office's barred roadway window. They spent at least a quarter of an hour watching but the stranger did not appear.

Sherm had given a description but it could have fitted about half the rangemen between Montana and the Mex border.

He wasn't too concerned anyway.

He had sent his telegram concerning his prisoner and the particulars on the robbery and shooting. Their association was about as it should have been between a lawman and a prisoner. He had no reason to be hard on a prisoner he was holding for extradition, one who, to Sherm's knowledge, had committed no crime in Sherm's territory, finally, a prisoner he had known for years and liked.

Travis didn't mention having sent for the fee lawyer, but when the tall, hard-eyed visitor who had preempted the rocking chair said his name was Garfield, Travis did some rethinking. The fee lawyer's name was Alex Rosen. He accepted the fact the stranger was a cattle buyer although it really was the wrong time of the year for buying.

If Will had been present when that alias was used he would have been able to identify his companion in the Deming robbery, but he was sleeping in his cell. For Travis and Garfield it was a short visit. Travis had no cattle ready to sell which was about all Garfield talked about.

In Culleyville, about a week after of the arrival of Garfield, the livestock buyer, two events occurred which heightened Culleyville's gossipy grapevine. Not only had another tight-mouthed stranger arrived in town but Lisbeth Deane received a telegram that her brother would be ready to stand the trip from Deming to Culleyville and would arrive home within the next week or so.

Folks were so interested in Al Burton's return they scarcely heeded the latest stranger. If it hadn't been that this visitor did not often patronize Boyard's waterhole, which in itself was notable since his attire clearly designated him as a stockman and of all the vices men possessed, saloons and livestock men went together.

Sherm encountered a stranger at the livery barn where a horse was being hayed and grained.

His name, he said, was Walt Carter and he was a surveyor by trade. Beyond that he volunteered little about himself but he seemed to the town marshal to be an individual who was capable of looking out for himself. It was entirely by accident that Sherm learned about the surveyor. They met at the livery barn. They exchanged greetings and Sherm noticed something. This surveyor wore his sidearm lower than was customary.

It was late afternoon when Sherm and the surveyor met for the second time. Sherm was riding out and the surveyor was heading in.

Where they stopped above the north perimeter of town there was a tawdry old leaning tree.

The surveyor opened the conversation with a statement that startled the town marshal. He was smiling when he said, 'It's my custom to do some horsebacking when I come to a territory I'm not familiar with. That goes for local law too, Marshal. I'm not a surveyor, I work for the Pinkerton people out of the Albuquerque office. You've heard of the Pinkertons?'

Sherm's reply was the truth. 'Everyone's heard of the Pinkerton Detective Agency, Mr Carter.'

The other man's smile lingered. Carter understood the way that reply was given. 'I was going to look you up in town.'

'Mind telling me why the Pinkertons are interested in Culleyville?'

'It's got to do with a stage robbery

down near Deming some time ago. The stage company hired us. There's some things that didn't seem right.'

'Is it a secret?' Sherm asked, and the other man's smile began to fade. 'No. Not exactly. I know the driver got shot an' he's coming here. His widowed sister lives here.'

Sherm loosened in the saddle. 'Lisbeth Deane. Her husband died some years back. Al Burton's the only family she's got left.'

Carter's nod left Sherm with the impression that Carter knew more than Sherm did. That impression was strengthened when the Pinkerton man also said, 'That Culley feller who escaped down from Deming's got a father hereabout too. Travis Culley, runs a good-sized cattle outfit. He's on my list of folks to talk to.'

'Is that why you're here? To run down Will Culley?'

'The reason I'm here, Marshal, has more to do with Deming than your town. That stage they stopped was

108

carrying fresh minted money. According to the Deming profile the money was missing when the coach reached Deming.'

'And you think the highwaymen took it?'

'We got reason to believe they didn't take it. Didn't even know it was bolted beneath the stage.'

'But it was gone?'

'Yes.'

'Mister Carter, I've got Will Culley in a cell at the jailhouse. If you want to talk to him you're welcome to.'

'Thanks, Marshal. Maybe in a day or two. Right now I'm lookin' for the other two.' Carter leaned on his saddle horn looking steadily at the town marshal. 'We suspect the Deming police let Culley and one of the others escape and gave them money to leave the country.'

'Mister Carter, just how much money was there?'

'Sixteen thousand dollars.'

Sherm's eyes widened. 'In a box under the coach?'

'It wasn't our idea, Marshal. They'd have saved a lot of money if they'd have just hired two Pinkertons to ride along. But that's water under the bridge. What I need is an hour or so with the highwaymen who escaped.'

Sherm raised his left hand with the reins in it. 'Ride along. You can talk to young Culley.'

As they headed for town, the Pinkerton man said, 'We've got two men in the Deming country. They already have suspects. With a little luck what I can learn up here will tie the calf down, as they say.'

Sherm was silent for most of the ride back. He had never before met a Pinkerton detective. He was familiar with the event that had made the Pinkertons famous. During the Civil War President Lincoln had hired Pinkerton agents as spies behind the Confederacy's lines. After the war, the United States had formed its own intelligence agency.

When they rode down the main

thoroughfare side by side tongues began to wag.

After leaving their animals with the liveryman they went up to the jailhouse where Sherm pointed to a chair, lifted a ring off a nail in the wall and went to get his prisoner.

Will looked up from his perch on the edge of the bunk bolted to the wall and watched the marshal unlock and open the cell door. Before taking young Culley to the office he explained his purpose, told him who would question him and led off.

Carter offered a hand, smiled and mentioned his name. Will did the same, went to the wall bench and sat down. The Pinkerton man remained standing. He was especially notable beyond the obvious fact that he was powerfully muscled and wore his belt-gun without a tie-down.

He asked questions which Will answered and the local lawman sat at his desk, hands clasped atop it, watching and listening.

Carter did not mention the money or where it had been hidden. He asked a number of other questions and when he was finished he was amiable. He sat and spoke in general. Neither Sherm nor Will had ever known a Pinkerton man and Sherm was favourably impressed.

Will had one question. 'Can Sherm hold me for something I didn't do in New Messico?'

The Pinkerton man's smile returned when he answered. 'That's up to him. If they send along extradition papers . . . Right now, I'd say he's holding you on suspicion. You three did stop that coach. Tell me something, Mr Culley, where can I find Taylor? I know Holding headed north from Deming. One more question: is there some reason why either or both would want to find you?'

Will hung fire over an answer so long Sherm looked long and hard at him.

Eventually young Culley answered in what both his listeners felt was not the truth.

'I got no idea where they'd go an' I got no idea why they'd look me up if that's what you're askin'. After we was caught I didn't see either of them.'

The Pinkerton man avoided the eyes of Sherm and young Culley long enough to dislodge a foxtail from a trouser leg then his head came up and he wasn't smiling.

'Tell me how you escaped, Mr Culley.'

For Sherm this seemed to be the point of Carter's desire to talk to Will Culley.

Will shot a glance in Sherm's direction before answering. 'There was a big fat Messican jailer . . . I'll make it short; he forgot to lock my cell. I waited until two o'clock in the morning then tiptoed out, caught me a horse an' left.'

6

'Ain't No Such Man'

Sherm had locked young Culley in his cell, he returned to his office and was surprised to find the Pinkerton man sitting comfortably smoking a quirly. He looked up smiling. 'Marshal. I think he told the truth.'

Sherm went to sit at his desk before answering. 'I've known him since I came here. He's not a liar. A damned fool, but not a liar. Mister Carter, if it's the law down in the Deming country who got that money an' set the captive highwaymen so's they could escape, why would they want to find my prisoner?'

Carter trickled smoke. 'I can guess; he's got something of theirs, or maybe that they think is theirs. One thing, Marshal, the one called Tex Taylor went south not north. Our agency had two men after him. But my idea is — either Taylor ran scairt or just wanted to get far off. Maybe Holding don't have much of a reason for trackin' Culley to here. You can't always know why outlaws do some things.' Carter killed his smoke. As he was straightening up the telegrapher walked in, eyeshade, sleeve garters and all. He nodded without speaking, dropped a piece of paper on the desk, nodded again and left the room.

Carter said, 'Talkative gent, isn't he?'

Sherm was reading the piece of paper and didn't answer. When he was finished he offered the paper.

Carter raised his head slowly. 'I just talked to Culley. The wireless from the Deming police says all the highwaymen have been caught an' the feller who got shot is on his way home.' Carter put the message back on Sherm's desk, went back to his chair, sat down and said, 'That last line about the Pinkertons calling the case closed . . . '

Sherm almost grinned. 'Maybe there's a telegram for you, tellin' you to come home.'

Carter sat without speaking for a moment then shot up to his feet. As he was leaving he said, 'If there is I'll let you know. But . . . are you plumb certain that's Culley you got in your cell?'

Sherm nodded his head. 'I've known him . . . I told you, I've known Will Culley since I cam here an' that's pushin' a number of years.'

Carter's stride in the direction of the telegraph office was wide and thrusting. Sherm returned from the window, sat down, and tugged his hat forward. This was not going to be his responsibility much longer. As the Pinkerton man had told him earlier, the real suspicion belonged several hundred miles southward.

The midday north-bound stage arrived at its corralyard about two in the afternoon, Lisbeth was up there waiting. When her brother alighted, two

116

yardmen got on each side and helped him to an old bench against the corralyard boss's office.

Sherm knew nothing of Burton's arrival until he saw Lisbeth walking past with two husky yardmen helping her brother.

He waited a discreet quarter of an hour before leaving the jail. The little house Lisbeth Deane had inherited when her husband died was wood all the way through. It badly needed oiling, there were cracks and bulges caused by warp.

She met Sherm at the door, wordlessly led him to her brother's bedroom and brought a chair. She obscured her brother when she leaned over the bed, but her brother had seen the marshal and said, 'Later, Sis. It'll hold off needin' a bandage change. Maybe Sherm'd like some coffee.'

After Lisbeth had gone, Al Burton said, 'I'll never ride another one of those old stages as long as I live. Why in hell don't they put those newfangled leather springs under 'em?'

That was a sore subject with the short-tempered stage company boss. It would be expensive and would take a rig out of circulation, but eventually Sherm was convinced thoroughbrace springs would replace the kind Burton was complaining about.

Sherm opened their visit with a stock remark. 'You look pretty good, Al. What'd they do for you in Deming?'

'Liked to killed me, those bone-sawing sons of bitches . . . Sherm?'

'Yes.'

'If it'd been a tad more to the right it would have busted my hip bone. I know why you're here. All I can tell you was that I was fightin' to hold the hitch steady. I didn't see him shoot. Where I fell from the seat to the ground knocked me plumb cold for a while. It was all over about the time they'd finished. Down yonder they'd asked every day did I see 'em. Every time I told 'em the gospel truth. I saw 'em only when they jumped out an' stopped the rig. I didn't remember what they looked like.'

Sherm accepted the cup of coffee from Lisbeth and thanked her.

She blocked the view again when she put some worn but immaculate towels on the little bedside table, rolled up her sleeves and didn't look around when she said, 'You hold him, Sherm. I could smell him from the doorway.'

Maybe she could but Sherm couldn't. As he arose, her brother tried to grip blankets which his sister was preparing to take away. Burton had the expression of a trapped animal.

Sherm said, 'Lisbeth, maybe we hadn't ought to do this.'

She turned on him with a fierceness he had never suspected she possessed. 'I'm going to wash him and give him a fresh bandage. You can smell it from the doorway. Sherm, help me or I'll hire a couple of those corralyard men.' Sherm went closer and looked down. Al Burton had a wide-eyed glassy stare.

He said, 'I'm fine. Don't let her

. . . she don't know anything about wounds an' bandagin'.'

Lisbeth roughly shouldered the town marshal aside. With her sleeves rolled up she looked capable enough. Sherm addressed her brother.

'I can smell it, Al. You likely got maggots in there. I got to hold you. I'm sorry.'

The man in the bed made a final plea. 'Sis, a man's got his privacy.' She was prying the blankets loose when she shocked the marshal. 'Al, I was married eleven years. Now lie still.' His sister went to work, frowning and efficient. Sherm helped until she told him to go sit down, he was in the way.

Her brother flinched twice and made a loud croaking sound when she used hot water to soften the bloodiest bandage. She ignored him.

When she eventually straightened back and wiped her hands she glared at the marshal. 'Throw that water out. Rinse the bowl and refill it from the kettle on the stove. *Now, Sherm!*'

Her brother strained around. Lisbeth said, 'It's healing.'

'They told me in Deming there'd be maggots. You see any?'

She lied with a clear conscience. 'Just small ones.'

Sherm returned, placed the big bowl on the little table and leaned to say, 'It don't look bad, Al.'

'Yeah; except for the maggots! Get rid of 'em, Sis.' Sherm leaned closer, frowning. When he started to say he saw no maggots Lisbeth jammed him in the ribs with an elbow.

The rebandaging preceded well enough. At least the patient neither squawked nor flinched. When it was finished Lisbeth said, 'Did you see who shot you?'

Her brother mopped sweat off his face with the corner of a flannel blanket as he answered. 'I didn't see much, the horses were raising hell.'

Before Sherm could stop her, she said, 'It was Will Culley.'

Her brother looked at Sherm as his

sister began gathering items to take to the kitchen. Sherm waited until she was gone before speaking. 'That's what the Deming police telegraphed us.'

'Will . . . ? He was one of the highwaymen? They told me that but I didn't believe it or pay much attention to their talk. I was in pain.'

Sherm grudgingly nodded.

'What was he doing down in the Deming country?'

'There were three of them, Al. Will was one.'

'I don't believe it.'

'I got him locked in jail. I'll bring him down here. He'll tell you.'

There was rapid, almost drum-like knocks on the roadside door.

The Pinkerton man was out there. He didn't smile when he spoke. 'One of 'em's here. Here in town. If it's not him it's the best likeness I've ever seen.'

Carter fumbled inside his coat, held up a tintype and waited for the marshal's reaction.

There was none. Sherm held the

photograph to the light, held it in shadows. The best he could do was discern the very dark and cloudy outline of a face and shoulders.

He handed back the tintype shaking his head. 'That could be anyone.'

Carter was putting the photograph in his pocket when he spoke again.

'It's real dark for a fact, but he uses the name Garfield. He's used it before. Some fellers at the saloon identified him. Garfield. That's his name up here. Marshal. I tell you that's Holding.'

'You're sure?'

'Plumb certain.'

'Let's go get him, if he's still at the saloon.'

'As near as I could find out he's left town. I went to his room at the hotel. I found something interesting. A scrap of paper from Durango. From the other one — Taylor. He's coming up here, Marshal. There's reason. Why would they congregate where the feller who was driving the coach ended up?'

Sherm briefly considered taking the

Pinkerton man inside for a talk with Lisbeth's brother, and decided not to. He told Carter he would be at the jailhouse directly and they could figure a way to apprehend the man calling himself Garfield.

Sherm took Lisbeth to the kitchen, told her what the Pinkerton man had to say, told her not to let anyone inside the house and left. On the way to the jailhouse he did some thinking. He was the law in the Culleyville territory, the initiative was his.

The Pinkerton man arrived and smiled, which indicated to the marshal that Carter's mood had changed. To prove this he limited their first few minutes together to asking simple questions, by saying things designed not to annoy the other man.

After an hour of conversation, Sherm decided that Carter might be right although it still bothered him about the tintype.

It came close to operating in reverse when the Pinkerton man said, 'He's

124

been asking a lot of questions, an' according to the liveryman he rode out an' was gone all day.'

Sherm hunched forward at his desk. 'You think he's huntin' for a cache?'

Carter was non-committal. 'I don't have a clear notion of what he's doing beyond him being here. How about that feller at the woman's house? Would he have an idea?'

'About the highwaymen bein' here? I don't think so but I'll ask. Mister Carter, I'd take it right kindly if you wouldn't go down there. He's doin' well. If you came calling it would surely upset him.'

'Can you do it, Marshal? Can you sweat it out of him?'

'I can sure try. But damned if I can figure him bein' involved with those highwaymen.'

After announcing that he had some horsebacking to do, Walt Carter not only left the jailhouse he also left the town. The few people who saw him leaving town remembered his course as being westward.

Sherm picked up that bit of information from the harness-maker who had been across the alley from his shop hoeing in his garden patch. He told Sherm the stranger looked like he might be one of those emigrating folk that usually sent a scout ahead.

Sherm nodded, returned to Lisbeth Deane's house and got a surprise. Al was sitting in a parlour chair with a robe covering as much of him as Lisbeth thought necessary.

Al was in good spirits as he greeted the town marshal. Sherm speculated about Burton's difference between the last time they had visited and the present time.

The mystery was resolved when Lisbeth brought Sherm a cup of coffee and took her brother's cup to be refilled. Sherm watched something being done at the kitchen drain board. Lisbeth tipped her brother's cup slightly and poured something into it. The bottle had a label.

Sherm got comfortable in a nearly ragged chair, waited until Al raised his cup in a slight salute and dropped the contents straight down.

Sherm sampled his drink. It was almost straight whiskey, maybe slightly weakened, he couldn't be sure, but within minutes Lisbeth's brother not only brightened but spoke freely.

He said he could recall things better today after he had been cleaned up, rested, comfortable after his long stage trip and of course the whiskey helped. He also said, he saw nothing, heard nothing, and couldn't remember being shot. What he could remember was the pain and being unable to stand up.

Sherm asked about the care he had received and that brought a recollection. 'The feller who worked on me was an army doctor. Gettin' handled by him was like bein' mauled by a bear.'

Lisbeth commented from the kitchen. 'But you're here, Al.'

There was no denying that but her brother threw her a glare nonetheless.

When Sherm declined having his coffee cup refilled and stood up to leave, the wounded man casually said, 'I never got it straight, when that sawbones took off the bandage he'd just put on no more'n ten minutes before an' helped me to the stage. Most likely it was my imagination but he treated me real fine all the way to the corralyard and helped me climb in. Like I was his kin or his friend, which, take my word for it, Sherm, wasn't how he treated me before.' Lisbeth's brother held aloft his empty little cup.

She came down on him like a load of rocks. 'You've had enough. That's the fifth one you've had since I helped you to the chair.'

Sherm watched Al Burton's expression turn from pleasant to sullen. He said, 'Maybe you'd got the bandage wet, Al.'

That remark brought a slight increase in the colour in Burton's face.

'Sherm, it's been forty years since I wet my pants. It wasn't that. Onliest thing . . . when he dropped the old bandage on the floor it dropped like a load of bricks.'

Sherm stood gazing at the man in the chair. 'Al, when he wrapped you in the new bandage, did it seem as heavy as the one he'd just removed?'

'All I know was that it hurt like hell if I lay on my back. I had a notion, him bein' a mean son of a bitch, he'd put stones in the bandage. It hurt like hell when I was on my back. That's why I mostly lay on one side or the other.'

'Al . . . '

'Sherm,' Burton said peevishly, 'I couldn't stand up, couldn't even get out of the bed without help.'

Sherm was motionless for a moment before lightly patting Al's shoulder and thanking Lisbeth for the java and left the house. He searched for Carter and was told by the harness-maker he had seen the stranger leave town heading west.

If Carter went west it was possible he might have in mind visiting with Travis

Culley, although Sherm could not imagine why. To his knowledge there would be no reason for the Pinkerton lawman to visit old Travis.

The following morning he met Walt Carter and began to form an idea. It was so unreasonable he discarded it without a second thought, except for one thing which he mentioned to no one.

At the telegrapher's office he did as he'd done once before. He waited until he was satisfied the message had been sent before taking breakfast over to his prisoner. They sat on the wall bunk making casual talk until young Culley had eaten, then Sherm took the tin cup and platter to his office and returned to the cell.

He offered the prisoner a sack of tobacco and the papers, waited until Culley had built and lighted a smoke, then said, 'What happened to that sixteen thousand dollars, Will?'

The prisoner looked up. 'I told you; they took it.'

'They knew it was in the stage's undercarriage?'

'Yes. Sherm, I already explained this. They had to know it.'

Sherm eased down on the edge of the bed. 'How did they know it was under there?'

For a moment or two young Culley stared, then straightened up to answer. 'They knew.'

'How?'

'Sherm, for Chris'sake . . . '

'Will, folks don't normally carry money under a rig like that. That's what bothers me, Will.'

Culley arose slowly without taking his gaze from the marshal. 'I got no idea how all this come about. They just plain knew where to look, an' that's the gospel truth.'

Sherm looked for a place to sit, saw a little stool, sat on it considering his prisoner.

Will expelled a long breath. 'Sherm, they stopped the coach. They didn't waste no time. All I know was how they went to the vehicle, got down on their knees an' went to work.' Will paused then added in an annoyed tone of voice. 'That's all I know, Sherm. They knew where to look.'

Young Culley eased back the tiniest bit staring at the town marshal and almost imperceptibly wagged his head. Sherm spoke again. 'They knew where the money was hid. They told you?'

'No, sir. They told me nothin', we just rode out there, set up the bushwhack an' when the rig come along they was ready.' Young Culley slowly arose, went to that small window and from over there spoke without facing around.

'I had no idea what was happenin' until a gun went off.'

Sherm was in the cell doorway blocking it when Culley said, 'Sherm, I come on to them two down at a Mex village called Gonzaga. We sort of hit it off.'

Will turned back facing into the room, briefly hesitated then returned to the wall bunk and perched on the edge of it. Culley said, 'There was three of 'em, but I only saw the two. We knocked back a few an' the one feller I didn't see left. Me'n the other two visited their camp, had a few more an' the next mornin' they showed me how they figured to catch that coach. There was no mention of that bullion box being underneath.'

'Any reason for it bein' that special stage, Will?'

'No. They told me nothin'. I was plumb surprised. You know the rest.'

'Two things I don't know Will: who got the money an' what happened to it?'

Sherm went to stand in the door-way. He was wearing a hard-twisted humourless little smile. 'Think back, Will. I'll be back. Right now I got a little chasin' to do.'

Young Culley was holding to the straps of the cell door when he called after the town marshal.

'If they'll come here, why? I don't

133

know anything about the money?'

Sherm paused long enough to say, 'I feel like a feller holding a sack with a hole in the bottom.'

Outside, Culleyville was going about its business the way it ordinarily did on a warm day. People, mostly women with shopping bags were going in and out of the general store the way they always did. Someone at the lower end of town was warping a hot shoe over an anvil, and near the upper end of town a man emerged from the saloon. It was the Pinkerton man. Sherm crossed over and started walking northward in the direction of the saloon.

He didn't make it. As he was passing the telegrapher's cubbyhole, the thin man rarely seen without a green eyeshade came to the doorway and made a conspiratorial gesture.

When Sherm was inside the telegrapher pointed to a rickety chair, went to his table with the telegraph key on it, picked up a pale yellow paper, took it over where Sherm was standing in front of the rickety chair and handed him the paper.

Sherm tipped his hat back, read the yellow piece of paper, looked up, looked down and reread the paper.

The telegrapher quietly said, 'You had a hunch, Marshal?'

Sherm was folding the paper before pocketing it when he answered. 'Not exactly, but sort of.'

'There's your answer. There ain't no Pinkerton detective assigned down here from either their Albuquerque office or from their headquarters up in Denver.'

7

Manhunt!

Travis Culley was sitting on his porch watching the rider approach. In mostly flat country a man could see for miles.

He called for Felice to take the marshal's horse. Felice was waiting when Sherm reached the yard, dismounted and held out the reins.

Felice said, 'He's on the porch. I'll off-saddle an' feed your horse.'

Sherm said, 'Thanks,' and was pulling off his gloves as he went toward the house.

Travis called a greeting and was ready to heave up out of the rocker and said, 'I'll get us some pop skull,' and got a quick response. 'Not for me, Travis.'

Travis settled back in the chair. Sherm did as he ordinarily did, he perched on the peeled-log porch railing.

Travis eyed the lawman thoughtfully before saying, 'That damned fee lawyer got hung up an' won't get down here for another week . . . How's Will holding up?'

'Pretty well for someone who's not used to being in a cage . . . Travis? Did you have a visitor within the last few days? His name's Carter. Walt Carter.'

The older man's expression changed. 'He come by. He's some kind of special lawman.'

'You mind tellin' me what you two talked about?'

'Don't mind at all. He's a Pinkerton special agent. I've heard of them over the years. This is the first time I ever seen one. We talked about Will, how he got into trouble down south. The stage company hired this Pinkerton outfit to find Will.' Travis leaned to expectorate over the peeled-log railing, settled back and fixed the marshal with a squinty-eyed look. 'We talked about the weather, about the price of cattle, how far it is to shipping pens. Things that folks in the livestock business talk about. He told me he used to be a cattle buyer. We talked about Will's predicament.' Travis leaned to jettison his cud of chewing tobacco and this time when he settled back he said, 'Sherm, I been countin' on that damned book lawyer.'

Sherm nodded. 'Will can stand it another week.'

'I expect so, only he don't deserve bein' locked up like a rabid wolf. Mister Carter agreed with me about that. You sure you wouldn't like a little Hiram Walker?'

'No thanks, Travis.'

'It's smooth whiskey.'

Sherm smiled. 'Get one yourself but count me out.'

The older man shot up out of his rocker and disappeared inside the house.

Sherm arose, leaned on the railing looking easterly. The view ran for miles. There was no movement, if there had been anyone on the porch could discern it.

The older man returned, sat in his rocker and exuded pleasantness. He'd had two jolts in the house. One for himself, the other one for his guest.

As he sat down he said, 'Sherm, it ain't right you holdin' Will because some law down in New Messico thinks he's an outlaw.'

Sherm agreed with that. They talked of little else than injustice and the stranger whose interest in Will was genuine, and that son-of-a-bitching fee lawyer.

Sherm left the Culley yard with a tint of red colouring the sky. It was a reasonably long ride back to town. He'd made other such rides and he had used them as he used this ride. For one thing speculating on Carter's visit to Travis, for which he could imagine no reason.

Not until he had the town lights in sight, then he did as he had done at other times, he selected parts, the most pertinent parts, of their lengthy conversation, rearranged them in his mind and came up with a startling possibility.

139

Carter was not a Pinkerton agent. Even if he had been one there would be no reason for him to make that long ride out and back to talk to Travis whom he would not know — unless Will had mentioned his father's name and where he lived.

When he reached town he got a surprise. Will'd had a visitor during Sherm's absence and the caller had made quite an impression.

The storekeeper across from the jail-house had mentioned a customer in need of tobacco asking questions about the town marshal's prisoner. All Christy could tell him was that the prisoner was Will Culley, son of Travis Culley whose land almost reached the town limits of Culleyville.

What troubled Sherm was that when he asked Will about the visitor, Will, initially anyway, denied he'd had a caller but later in a burst of anger, said, 'Why in hell don't you lock this place up when you're goin' to be gone? His name is Holding. Art Holding. He

140

tracked me here an' you got to turn me loose.'

'Why?'

'Because him'n another feller are goin' to kill me.'

Sherm sat in the cell on the small stool considering the overwrought anxiety of his prisoner. For a fact he would lock the jailhouse tight after this. He asked who the other man was who wanted to kill Will and got a loud answer. 'That damned Texan. A few swallows of rot gut an' he goes crazy.'

'They were the fellers you stopped the stage with?'

'Yes. There was another feller. They told me he high-tailed it to Messico.'

'Will, calm down. They aren't — '

'You don't know them, Sherm.'

'All right. Why do they want to kill you?'

'Because they think I made off with some of the money an' we was to divide it even.'

'Will . . . did you?'

Young Culley made a wild gesture

with both arms. 'I already told you, I didn't know there was any money. Nobody told me about the cache nor how much there was. But I can tell you one thing for a cinch, Sherm, somebody got that money an' it wasn't Taylor or Holding, or they wouldn't have tracked me down believin' I got it.'

Someone rattled the roadway door. Sherm locked his prisoner in before returning to his office. His caller was Lisbeth Deane. Two men had called to see her brother. She told them he was sleeping and couldn't be disturbed. She told Sherm they tried to push their way past and her brother was in the bedroom doorway with a six-gun in his hand. She said they called her brother by name and said they would be back, and left.

Lisbeth told Sherm she had never seen either of those men before. She also said she was afraid.

He soothed her, promised to come by and visit with her brother directly and sent her home with an admonition.

'Use your pa's old scattergun, I saw it leanin' in the kitchen.'

After Lisbeth departed, Sherm returned to the cell. He told Will what he thought. 'It's your two friends. I'll make a guess, they think Al's involved with the money they stole and someone stole from them.'

Will scoffed. 'How could he have got the money, he was shot, remember?'

Later, when Sherm arrived at the Deane house, Al Burton was jockeying into the least painful position. When he saw Sherm he said, 'I'll tell you again: I know nothin' about the money. Nothing! Not a damned thing! Until the medicine man was workin' on me an' I heard some arguin' I didn't know about the damned sixteen thousand dollars. Sherm, that's the gospel truth. If anyone in this territory knows anythin' about the damned money it's got to be Will.'

Lisbeth stood in the bedroom doorway. She was pale. While twisting a small, fragile lace handkerchief she said,

'Sherm. who were those two men? I'm afraid to think what would have happened if Al hadn't heard them.' She looked at her brother. 'You shouldn't have got out of bed.' She went to bedside and reached to peel back the covers. Her brother, already in an agitated frame of mind, resisted.

She stepped back toward Sherm. 'I want to see if he's bleeding.'

Sherm stepped close, used one hand and lowered the covers.

There was no sign of blood.

Sherm put the covers back and blew out a long sigh. 'Al . . . ?'

'I got no idea, Sherm. I'm beginnin' to think everybody's after that money an' I swear to Gawd I got no idea who got it or where it is. Sherm? You're the law!'

Sherm left the house, made an angry search of the town for a pair of strangers and for the second time in the same day failed to even find the Pinkerton man.

He returned to the jailhouse and

went to work doing something he'd been putting off for weeks. He took each weapon from the wall rack, dug out his cleaning equipment and went to work. One of the shotguns had a cobweb in it. The spider rode the cleaning rod all the way out. Sherm flicked it away and went back to work. He had cleaned two saddle guns, a pair of pistols and was working on the last weapon, a scattergun, when two men walked in, and stopped stone still. Sherm was sitting with the reloaded and cleaned shotgun in both hands.

One of the men addressed his companion. 'This ain't a good time. We can come back later.'

Sherm wigwagged with the shotgun. 'Set, gents. I'm about through.'

They sat. One looked familiar, but Sherm couldn't place him. The other one was more of a stranger to him. It was this one who waited until Sherm had replaced the shotgun in its niche and returned to the desk before speaking.

'You'll be the town marshal.'

Sherm nodded, leaned back off the desk and decided his visitors were rangemen. They were dressed the part. He broke the silence by asking what he could do for the strangers and one of them, leaner, more weathered than his companion drew his six-gun without haste and said, 'You can bring up your prisoner an' turn him over to us.'

Sherm did not move. Silence settled. It was eventually broken by the man who hadn't spoken. He said, 'We're not jokin', Marshal. You just set there with your hands atop the table while my partner takes them keys and fetches your prisoner. We got business with him. You just set real easy.'

They were both tall men, the one who looked older, was a tad taller. He held that six-gun like someone who was at home holding the thing.

He said something aside to his partner and was poised to cross to the desk when someone rattled the door twice then lifted the latch from the

146

outside and walked in.

It was Travis Culley. He looked from Sherm to the strangers and said he'd come back later. Sherm said, 'You're welcome. We were just talkin' about Will. These fellers knew him down south.'

Travis faced the younger and taller men. 'It's my son he's got locked up, gents. For no reason except someone in New Messico got a charge against my boy for stopping a stage down there some place.'

The youngest of the strangers smiled and nodded in Travis's direction. He had the expression of a man balancing on the edge of a hard decision. His companion had leathered his Colt but kept his hand close to it.

Travis said, 'You boys friends of Will? Well, come home with me after you visit. Friends of my boy is friends of mine.'

The taller and older man made a sickly smile. 'That's right decent of you, Mr Culley, but me'n my partner here

147

figured to head south right after supper.'

Travis turned his attention on Sherm. 'Is he doin' well? He ain't lookin' sickly is he? Us Culleys never could stand bein' cooped up for long.'

One of the strangers moved quietly, got behind Travis, dropped the draw bar into its hanger, which effectively locked the roadway door from the inside, and gently pushed his six-gun barrel into Travis's back. When Travis stiffened without moving, his holster was emptied and he was shoved toward the wall bench.

As he sat down Sherm shook his head. 'Walked right into it, Travis.'

'How'n hell was I to know?'

The older man tossed Sherm's ring of keys to his partner and jerked his head. 'Get him out an' bring him up here.'

As the younger stranger moved to obey, his partner addressed Travis. 'You're his pa. Tell me somethin': has he come out to your home place since he got back?'

Travis's face was set in an expression of hostility when he answered. 'He come home. That's where he mostly grew up.'

The older stranger exchanged a look with the younger stranger and spoke again to Travis. 'An' what'd he do when he got home?' At Travis's blank look the older man also said, 'I mean, did he have saddle-bags or somethin' like that, an' if he did where did he hide 'em?'

Travis considered the speaker, flicked a glance at Sherm and spoke. 'All's I can tell you is he just sort of settled in. He'd been gone quite a spell.'

'What did he bring with him? Old-timer, him 'n' some others robbed a stage an' run for it, got caught an' your boy escaped. He come here. What we want to know is, did he hide somethin'?'

'Not to my knowledge,' Travis exclaimed. 'Are you talkin' about bullion or what?'

'Cash in greenbacks. It's sort of an

involved story but we figure he got the money an' run with it.'

Travis surprised the town marshal, he showed an expression of dumbfounded amazement. 'We was together at the ranch. If he'd cached somethin' I'd have known it.' Travis looked from one man to the other. 'You fellers sure you're after the right man? A few days back a stranger visited me at the ranch. He was askin' pretty much the same questions you fellers been askin'.'

This time it was the youngest stranger who spoke. He said, 'Arthur, I told you: he got a head start on us comin' up here.'

The taller man called Arthur glared at his partner. 'We know that for Chris'sake, Tex.'

The younger man turned toward Travis. 'If it's hid it'll be somewhere close to home.'

Arthur jerked his head and said, 'Fetch him.'

The man in the office could plainly hear the astonishment in Will Culley's voice when Tex unlocked the cell door and ordered him to come out.

Tex prodded Will from behind. Nevertheless Will stopped dead still when he faced the men in the office, all glaring back at him. Will addressed his father. 'I've got nothin' they want, Pa.'

Travis's reply was laconic. He said, 'Well, Son, someone has an' if you know who I'd say tell 'em to hand it over.'

The man named Arthur suddenly growled at his companion. 'I told you, Tex; I told you ten times: It's got to be that whip, the one who drove the rig.'

Tex seemed baffled for the first time. 'All right. We can go back down there. But what'll we do with this bunch?'

Arthur jerked his head. 'Lock' 'em in their own cell.'

It was a good suggestion and Arthur moved to implement it by using his belt-gun as a prod. As they were entering the cell, Travis made them a cash offer, which they refused. He then

151

made threats and that did not seem to bother them.

After the cell door was locked, the tallest one said, 'We'll take Will with us an' for his sake he better have a good memory.' The speaker faced young Culley. 'Back alley, Will. Lead us down to where the whip's sister's takin' care of him.'

After their captors had departed Sherm removed a brass jailhouse key from a pocket, held it aloft where it was greeted with silence before he went to the door, jockeyed around until he could get his hand holding the key past the steel straps and had to strain to get his hand with the key in it, cocked plumb around and inserted.

There was not a sound as Sherm worked the key, up and down, from side to side, and sprung the lock. He let it fall and kicked the door open.

When they were in the office sorting out which sidearm belonged to whom, old Travis nudged the marshal. 'You always carry a spare key, Sherm?'

'Always, Travis, since my first year as a lawman an' some drunk rangemen locked me in my own jail. Travis, take that scattergun. I just cleaned an' reloaded it.'

When they were ready to leave the jailhouse, the roadway door was swung inward and Will Culley stood in the doorway without moving. Without even seeming to be breathing.

Will Culley moved to the side and the two highwaymen who had escaped and taken Will with them marched in, heads down trailed by Lisbeth Deane holding her pa's old scattergun.

Will kicked the door closed and shoved the speechless men toward Sherm.

'They're yours. Lock the sons of bitches up. We can take care of them later.' He turned to the two highwaymen and said, 'The gospel truth is that I don't have any of that money an' I got no idea where it is.'

Before one of the highwaymen could speak, Sherm grabbed the back of his collar and took him along with the other prisoner down to the cell and locked them in.

Lisbeth turned around and left the jailhouse heading in the direction of her house.

They had a brief palaver in the office, decided one of them would go to Lisbeth Deane's place and sit with her brother. Old Travis frowned. 'How many of them are there?'

Sherm's reply was short. 'That one who's supposed to be a Pinkerton man, Travis, but it won't hurt to round up every stranger'n bring 'em down here too.'

Travis still frowned. 'An' where's this money they're all after?'

Sherm supplied another answer. 'I can pretty well tell you where it is.'

'Where, Sherm?'

'Down in Deming. The authorities down there . . . this was their scheme from the start. They just didn't expect things'd get so badly out of hand.'

Travis eyed a chair but did not go

over and sit on it. He instead asked another question. 'Sherm? The law down yonder knew the money was comin'?'

Sherm nodded. 'They knew, an' they knew it'd be in a bullion box bolted beneath the stage. That's for someone else to unravel. Right now we got to see if there's another highwayman trailed Will an' Al Burton up here believin' one or both of 'em stole the money from the thieves an' high-tailed it for home up here with it, and find Walk Carter.'

Travis sounded exasperated when he said, 'How in hell could they figure Al had anything to do with it? He'd been shot.'

Sherm reset his hat and went to the roadway door and said, 'First, we make certain Al's safe. Then we start at the north end of town an' work our way southward on both sides of the road.' He opened the door and growled. 'Lastly, we bring Carter up here to the office and shellack him until he fills in the blind spots. Let's go, gents.'

Will stopped in the doorway. 'I'll go set with Al.'

No one argued. It had been common knowledge for years that Will Culley was sweet on Al's sister.

8

Getting Close. Too Close

For Sherman Kandelin, as with other lawmen, spare time was when he could sort through pertinent things and discard items that lacked immediate importance.

Deming was a considerable distance from his town and its territory.

He was satisfied how things for which Deming lawmen were responsible had to be handled that far from Culleyville.

It would not be the first, nor the last time lawmen succumbed. All he could do was give what proof he would eventually turn up that everything having to do with the planning and execution of the highway robbery and the loss of $16,000 originated in Deming. Beyond that whatever action should be taken was the responsibility of Deming's authorities.

He and Travis started their manhunt at the northern end of town. Will would be at the lower end. Sherm had originally thought there would be someone accompanying Will to guard Al and his sister, but that hadn't been possible, so it was Travis on the west side manhunting southward and the town marshal making the same sweep from the east side of the road. He wasn't hopeful. Until Walt Carter turned out to be something different from what he had represented himself to be, Sherm had begun to seriously consider the possibility that $16,000 might turn out to be a greater temptation than he might have thought. He was reasonably certain that money never left Deming and, in fact, after the passage of so much time the real thieves had probably divvied it and had flown the coop which meant Culleyville's town marshal was left holding a bag for which there would be no reward at his end.

For Travis his first visit resulted in no luck. The harness-maker hadn't seen anyone resembling the man Travis described, launched into a talkative tirade.

While Travis was struggling to disengage himself without being rude, across the road the town marshal was being told by the local gunsmith, who was also a locksmith, that he knew Carter by sight but hadn't done any business with him.

It was something less than a promising start.

Sherm's next stop was at Boyard's saloon and because the hour of his visit was not auspicious for his purpose, there were only four patrons who remembered Carter and one man claimed to have seen the individual the marshal sought around town no more than an hour or such a matter earlier.

By the time the search reached the lower end of town Travis had come up with nothing and Sherm had only the information supplied at the saloon and except for one patron up there stating when he had seen the wanted man Carter had been leaving town by the southernmost road, and that had been one or more hours before Sherm had appeared looking for him.

They returned to the jailhouse and got the surprise of their lives, while they had been manhunting and the jailhouse had been unattended someone had walked in, taken the key ring off its wall peg and had freed the prisoners.

Travis stood by the small barred roadway window looking out as he said, 'Will, they will have gone after him and taken him with 'em. You know what that means, Sherm? They'll roast his bare feet in a fire until he tells them where the money is hid, an' for a damned fact he don't know.'

Sherm was standing beside the older man softly nodding when someone using considerable force slammed the roadway door open so hard it went all the way back and struck the wall.

Alfred Lewis, the banker, was wild-eyed. 'He come in like anyone would have, kicked the roadway door closed, turned the card that says Closed an' got behind the counter to take the money from the clerk's drawer. Marshal, it'll ruin the bank. The funds he took aren't replaceable. *Marshal! The bank'll be ruined!*'

Travis turned slowly. 'Every account, Mr Lewis?'

'Mister Culley, every account, yours included.'

Sherm recovered slowly. The banker sank down on an empty bench. Travis went over and tapped the banker who looked up. Travis said, 'Did they open the safe, Alfred?'

'Yes, sir, Mr Culley. They got it all.'

'How much, Alfred?'

'Thirty-one thousand dollars, Mr Culley. Maybe a little more.'

Travis left the jailhouse without a word. Sherm followed, neglecting to lock up. Now, there was no reason to. The only person still in there was the banker; he was slumped over with his face in both hands.

Travis didn't reach his livery barn objective. The liveryman was mid-way when Travis met him. Before Travis could speak, the liveryman said, 'They taken my best horses, the bastards.'

'Which way'd they go?'

The liveryman turned with a rigidly raised arm. 'South, right straight south down the road.'

Travis seized the other older man. 'Saddle our horses, *right damned now!*'

Sherm stepped clear and looked southward. The midday stage was raising dust about a mile southward. Sherm went inside to rig his own mount. Travis was not quite ready when Sherm left the barn, reined southward and rode directly in the centre of the road, facing the oncoming stage. Sherm raised his left hand in a high wave. The stage driver kicked his binders while simultaneously leaning back on the lines. One of his passengers squawked when he was knocked off his seat.

Sherm was talking to the whip when Travis caught up. Sherm booted his mount over into a high lope. Behind him Travis yelled as the coachman eased off his binders and talked up his horses.

Sherm kept his lead. Travis could not come abreast until Sherm halted at a turn-off studying the ground. When the older man came up Sherm said, 'Dead ahead,' and led off.

An hour later they could see a dust banner where flat land began to yield to an upland slope. Sherm slackened his gait. Travis swore and would have hastened ahead up the slope but Sherm blocked him. 'No sense in wearin' 'em down, Travis.'

They alternated gaits from a fast walk to a high lope and when they topped out on a wide mesa, to a run.

Travis was impatient; it was difficult for him to ride stirrup with a town marshal who would not make a horse race out of the pursuit, but he was a lifelong horseman and understood the need for more endurance and less speed, but having lost a lifetime of savings was a powerful incentive to hasten.

Sherm raised his right arm. About a mile or maybe a tad more there were horsemen sitting on a ledge watching their back trail.

Travis said, 'I don't see Will.'

Sherm answered calmly. 'He's there. Count 'em. There's Carter, those two fellers from Deming and Will. Count 'em, Travis.'

Whether the older man counted them or not, the distant riders turned and were lost sight of down the far side of the high hill.

A mile further along with both pursuers watching tracks, Travis said, 'I know this country. Come within an ace of buyin' it years back.'

'Why didn't you?'

'Well, it's owned by some Easterners who come out once to see what they'd bought, an' never come back. There used to be a Mex town dead ahead about two miles. There's water an' plenty of places for 'em to make a stand.'

Sherm considered the landforms ahead. 'You know this country pretty well, Travis?'

'I just told you. Yes, I know it. As long as they leave sign we can find 'em. I'd like to do it before long; I'm gettin' hungry.'

Sherm was also hungry, but hadn't thought about it until Travis mentioned it. He said, 'Is there a way to get around an' come in on that village from the south? Some direction they won't be watchin' too hard?'

Instead of answering, old Culley left the road and rode along the slope of another sidehill. They eventually came to a bosque of trees; some were respectfully tall, most of the others were smoke-colored spruces, not as tall but a lot thicker.

They were tipping downslope when Travis said, 'I sure hope they'll stop at that old village. If they don't, if they keep goin', we'll be ridin' tired horses before they will.'

Sherm said little. He was concentrating on scanning ahead of Travis. It was not easy. They eventually had to dismount and lead their animals and the slower they had to go the more Travis Culley fidgeted.

He made one comment, eventually. 'Partner, it'll be dark at the rate we're goin',' and remounted.

They soon left the trees behind and Travis's mood seemed somewhat improved.

Without any warning, a pair of burros came up the trail toward them. They slid to a halt, hesitated very briefly and turned off the trail ducking and dodging as animals would only do if they knew the country.

Sherm halted, looked up at Travis and waited. The older man understood, dismounted, and they both walked ahead at the shoulders of their mounts; horses had a habit of trumpeting when they caught the scent of other horses.

Travis brushed the younger man's sleeve and spoke in a subdued tone. 'Up ahead, maybe a quarter-mile, there's a crop-out that overlooks the village.'

Sherm nodded. 'You're sure it's abandoned?'

'Has been since I came here. Some kind of sickness killed off half an' the other half moved out.'

Sherm came out of tall scrub brush and trees atop a tiny mesa. Below were what remained of what had once been a tidy small settlement. A creek passed through on the west side.

His heart sank. There was no sign of life, two-legged or four-legged. Travis said, 'What'n hell did you expect? They'll have hid their animals in one of those shacks.'

Sherm squatted in front of his horse. Shortly now daylight would begin to fade and in this kind of country tree tops would hasten the process of limited visibility.

He abruptly reached for Travis's

sleeve and pointed without making a sound.

Down below where sunlight still reached, a tall man was pitching armloads of dry feed into one of the *jacals*.

Travis hunkered. 'Recognize him?'

Sherm stifled his annoyance. At the distance between the hayfeeder and up where the pair of pursuers were squatting a man would not be able to recognize his own mother. Instead of replying to the question the town marshal said, 'Travis, from here on we got to do this on foot.'

Travis did not respond, but his attitude said clearly doing anything on foot that could be accomplished otherwise was outright idiocy.

They remained stationary until Sherm arose, moved back away from the drop-off, then led his horse in search of a suitable place to leave it. Travis did the same. Where they left the animals was in a one acre clearing where they could crop grass hopefully until their riders returned.

Sherm quartered for nearly a half-hour before he found a suitable trail down from the drop-off. Like the village below, the trail had once been frequently used but it too had fallen on hard times.

Sherm considered the increasing shadows as being mostly favourable although they were passing through rattlesnake country if he had ever scented one.

At the lower elevation there were plenty of stumps but no trees. The underbrush flourished though and they took every advantage of it to get down almost to the mesa with its abandoned houses, a few made of sturdy logs, the others made of adobe.

The sun was slanting away, its slow and ponderous passing left the village half in light, half in shadow.

The last place they hunkered was surrounded by flourishing thickets of thorn tree underbrush, some of the stands were man-tall.

Travis reconnoitered by crawling. Sherm raised just his head. They had several mud houses less than forty feet onward. Sherm wanted them to be empty. Travis returned from his scout to report that those houses were not only empty but so were the other hutments within reach.

While that pleased the older man it bothered Sherm for the possibility that while they'd been getting down there the men they sought might have struck camp. One thing was a certainty, they would not stay in one place any longer than they absolutely had to.

The almost haunting stillness was broken by a man raising his voice. 'By now they'd ought to be ten miles southward.'

An answer came back, tartly, 'If they ain't, you yellin'll get 'em comin'.'

'Aw, for Chris'sake don't be so jumpy.'

Travis jutted his jaw to indicate which *jacal* the talk had come from, and Sherm agreed. They got east until one of the nearby houses shielded them, then sprinted to the house and entered through a rear doorless opening.

Whoever had lived in this house had taken everything with them that could be carried, and subsequent residents with four feet and long bony tails had left an abundance of evidence of their lengthy visit.

The doorway facing westerly lacked a door. Sherm passed toward the front, leaned and waited. Travis came up and jutted his jaw again. 'That house yonder?'

Sherm nodded in silence. As they stood, shadows lengthened. Sherm wrinkled his nose. There was no smoke arising from the house they watched but the unmistakable aroma of cooking crossed the intervening distance.

Travis sighed. 'My belly thinks my throat's been cut. Let's hurry up about this, Sherm.'

The younger man could have been deaf. He neither spoke nor straightened up from his slouch.

Somewhere up above in the vicinity of that bluff where they had squatted, a coyote sounded. Minutes later the call was answered but from a greater distance.

Sherm wagged his head. It was getting late for mating. The pups would be born during the snowy season. Mother Nature didn't encourage late matings but then coyotes, like two-legged creatures, ignored Mother Nature when they had the urge.

Shadows were fully down when a man appeared, gathered deadfall twigs and returned to the house. He hadn't quite got inside when another man said, 'Walt, we got to be movin', hadn't we?'

'Yeah, directly.'

Sherm straightened up, hesitated long enough to address his companion then began moving through semi-darkness in the direction of the opening through which the kindling gatherer had disappeared.

Sherm paused just long enough to

yank loose the tie-down thong and fist his holstered Colt. As he approached the door, Travis made a loud gasp. Sherm turned as Travis went down and a gun exploded in the darkness from the direction of a small building.

Sherm's grip loosened, his handgun fell. He clung to consciousness for seconds before also dropping.

A man appeared in the doorway backgrounded by a small cooking fire some distance behind him. He was holding a twin-barrelled shotgun in both hands. He said, 'Tex, what in the hell . . . '

'They was creepin' toward the door.'

'Who are they?'

'Hell, I don't know. Help me flop 'em over.'

'I'll be gawddamned! It's the marshal. I don't know who the older one is.'

'I do. That's Will's pa . . . Travis Culley.'

Another man pushed through and was also backgrounded by the cooking fire. He leaned slightly, flopped Travis over by an arm and straightened up grinning. 'Fetch Will. That there's his pa.'

The man who had come from the distant small building wagged his head. 'I seen 'em stalkin'. It wasn't none of us so it had to be . . . '

'The old one's comin' around. Get his damned gun. The marshal's gun too.'

A third man pushed his way past the door. He stopped stone still as Travis struggled to get up onto all fours. The last man to leave the house roughed his way through, stood briefly then knelt to help Travis arise. It wasn't a success. Travis had been struck from behind with a solid steel pistol barrel. He fell back, rolled and tried again. This time the kneeling man caught him under both arms and lifted.

Travis's legs would not bear the weight until his son said, 'Hold still.'

The man who had caught Travis from behind started ahead snarling. Will got between them with one arm supporting his father. 'Leave him be!'

A man mostly in darkness jerked his head. 'Get 'em inside.'

Travis's legs were firming up. He still required the help of his son. They had the hardest time passing through the doorway.

The town marshal was half dragged, half carried. He was the heavier of the two not entirely because unconscious people are dead weight, but also because he was a large, massively muscled individual.

The *jacal* was smoky despite having a door and window that were blank holes. It was also hot. The cooking fire was bright in one of the corner burning areas used for both heating and cooking. It was not a large room.

Someone had found three stools, otherwise the house was devoid of furniture.

There was a Spanish name daubed in black on one wall with the year of abandonment.

The tall, weathered man leaned. 'He's dead.'

'Can't be,' the man who had fired outside said. 'I didn't aim, I just shot one off to let you know they was out there.'

The tall man leaned further, raised his hand for the others to see by firelight.

His fingers were covered with blood.

9

Win or Lose

Travis groaned until his son let him tip up a bottle, then he coughed and someone laughed. The same man said, 'He's got a skull of solid bone.'

The tall, weathered man was interested in Sherm. He grunted from the effort of getting the town marshal into a sitting position with a leg propping him. Walt Carter said, 'Where's he hit?' and got a reply tinged with astonishment. 'Alongside the head. I never miss at that range.'

'You sure it's a graze? He's bleedin' like a stuck hawg.'

The tall man jockeyed the marshal around until he was propped against a wall, stood up and wiped his hands on a bandanna. He muttered to himself while regarding the town marshal. 'At that distance for Chris'sake . . . '

Carter said, 'It's dark out there. An' as you said, you was just shootin' off a round. Try some of that coffee.'

As the tall man moved toward the stove Carter addressed him again.

'Art, now don't take me wrong but are you sure it's thirty-one thousand dollars? That damned place didn't look to me like it could scrape up ten thousand.'

The tall man turned and snarled. 'Count it yourself. It's in them saddle-bags.'

The younger renegade fidgeted, raised his head as though listening and said, 'They could be gettin' close. I favour gettin' astride and on the way. This darkness ain't goin' to last much longer.'

The tall man holding his hands to the fire agreed. 'I know what you're thinkin', Carter, but they found us, didn't they?'

That statement settled it, the bank thieves did not bother dousing the fire, they gathered their things and went out to the horses.

In the pine-scented darkness, a squeaky, somewhat unsteady voice said, 'You boys see a pair of burros? one's got more grey on him than — '

The gunshot reverberated. In its momentary flash of light it was possible to see the hidden man cocking his sidearm for another shot.

He got it off, the surrounding trees and brush choked back some of the sound.

The hidden man's second shot threw out a backlash of flame and another renegade also fired.

For several moments it was a brush fire-fight. The youngest outlaw straddled a bridled horse in one prodigious leap and bent low as he sank in his spurs. The frightened animal responded with one great leap before heading southerly dodging trees.

There was one more gunshot. It came from the north-east, its muzzle blast only lasted a second.

The period of silence was abruptly broken by the loud snort of a terrified horse striking a forest giant head on. The animal fell backwards, sprang up and fled southward stirrups flapping.

Travis dragged himself to the doorway. A shadow in night gloom whose back was to the door whirled. Both guns fired simultaneously. A silver of adobe doorjamb flew inward as far as where the town marshal was regaining consciousness.

The man who had fired in the darkness went down and stayed down.

Travis looked back, saw Sherm beginning to move and yelled at him, 'Come up here, boy!'

The man who was called after his area of origin yelled for Walt Carter. Instead of a reply he was fired at. He fell and rolled once.

Will yelled into the night, 'You better call it quits, or won't be one of you ride away . . . I'm waitin'.'

Old Travis came half out of his

crouch. 'Will? Stay down, boy.'

Sherm came up behind the elder Culley, who said, 'It's all over, near as I can tell . . . Will?'

'What?'

'You all right, boy?'

'I'll make it. I think the money's in the saddle pockets of the feller who run.'

Sherm arose, stood a moment looking and listening. He spoke, but not very loud. 'Mind the store. I know about where that horse hit the tree. Travis? Mind my back.'

Will moved, otherwise he could have been invisible. His father went as far as the riddled door and leaned there peering into darkness in the direction Sherm had taken.

An unsteady voice spoke from out in the night. 'If it's finished?'

Travis raised his fisted six-gun as he said, 'Which one are you? Walk toward the house where I can see you. No guns, or I'll blow your head off. Come on!'

The shadow that appeared in speckled moonlight held the men in the doorway motionless.

The man was old with an unkempt beard. He was not very tall, his clothing was patched and soiled. He had a holstered old hawgleg pistol, Army issue, on the right side.

Travis said, 'Drop that cannon, mister. Who in hell are you?'

'Names don't matter,' the wizened man replied. 'I prospect for minerals for miles around. Them two burros belong to me. When I set 'em loose to scavenge they always end up comin' over here. Who are you gents an' what you doin' out here?'

Travis left the old elfin-appearing prospector and went to look for Sherm. Will told the old man to get inside by the fire. When visibility was marginally improved, Will made a clucking sound. 'You come along just at the right time, mister.'

Travis appeared in the doorway with Sherm. The old man stared at Sherm's bloody shirt and torn scalp. He told Sherm where to sit and using a wicked-bladed boot knife removed the left sleeve from Sherm's shirt. There was no water to cleanse the wound; he went to work without no more than wiping it clean, then, using the rest of the shirt sleeve, tied it around Sherm's head.

When he was finished he reared back, pinched his eyes nearly closed and said, 'I've done better.'

Travis was looking at Sherm who had a world-beating headache. Sherm saw the look he was getting and spoke. 'You saw him, Travis. Broke his neck when the horse hit the tree.'

Travis's gaze did not waver. 'I saw him. Deader'n a stone. Where are the saddle-pockets? He had 'em on his saddle.'

Sherm sank to the floor and did not heed the old prospector who was working on him. Only once did they exchange words, that was when the old man said, 'For Gawd's sake hold still!

This here's a hard place to tie a bandage.'

'Where did you learn doctorin', mister?'

'In the Confederate Army. I was a cut'n sew man. Now be quiet an' don't flinch.'

Travis saw his son watching Sherm being doctored. Will said, 'Pa, are you sure the pouches was on the same horse that feller was ridin'?'

'Sure as I can be in the damned dark with a band of renegade sons of bitches tryin' to kill me.' He faced the old prospector.

'Why did you buy in, mister?'

'Some idiot seen me and fired. I had a better sighting and put him down for all time.' Travis considered the old man in silence for a moment then wagged his head and spoke again. 'What's your name, mister?'

The old man went on working over Sherm. 'Bernabe Swift, what's yours?'

'Travis Culley. That there is my son Will Culley. That there's the town marshal up yonder a piece. His name's Sherman Kandelin. Them deceased gents . . . I'm not sure they even got names. Sherm, what become of them saddle-bags?'

Sherm almost shook his head. Old Bernabe Swift held him in a vice-like grip. Sherm answered in that position. 'I got no idea.'

'That feller run into a tree an' is dead out there. So where's the saddle-pockets?'

'Travis . . . I didn't see the saddle-bags.'

'They didn't up an' walk away, Sherm.'

'Maybe one of those bank robbers got 'em an' got away.'

'No such a damned thing, Sherm. Count 'em. They're all accounted for.'

Will addressed his father whose voice had been getting shriller by the moment. 'They got to be around somewhere, Pa.'

Travis replied drily, his gaze still fixed on the town marshal. 'That's a fact,

185

boy. They're around somewhere. Maybe hid so's someone can come back an' get 'em.'

Sherm's colour mounted. He did not waver before the older man's stare, nor did he speak. Will spoke. 'Come on, Pa. You and me'll scout 'em up.'

Travis went with his son but his expression remained suspicious and grim.

The fire was burning low. Bernabe Swift had to work up close. As he did this he asked questions. When Sherm stated the amount of missing money the old man missed a stroke in his bandaging.

'There was . . . how much did you say?'

'Thirty-one thousand dollars.'

'Good Lord a'mercy. In Culleyville? Sonny, I've known that place since Hector was a pup. A man had that kind of wealth could've bought the town an' ever'thin' in it for half that much.'

The old man stepped back as he'd done before, squinched up his eyes and

186

passed judgement on the lawman.

'I've done better. Now you stay in here where it's warm. I'll go he'p them other two. Like someone said, it's got to be around.'

Sherm's head throbbed. The graze hadn't been as close as Sherm thought. It didn't have to be. Any torn hide up alongside a man's cranium bled for all it's worth.

Sherm probed gingerly and made a discovery no one had mentioned. He had a notch of meat missing from the top of his left ear.

Travis returned first and his answers to the questions were bitten off. 'No! We didn't find it. Will's goin' to stay out there and keep lookin.' Where's the old man?'

'Went to help search, Travis.'

'Why that old scruffin' son of a bitch,' Travis exclaimed and headed for the door.

Sherm fed the fire, lay flat out and closed his eyes. When he opened them it was bright daylight and out back a horse nickered.

Travis sank down near the town marshal. He may have been ashamed of himself, or he may simply have been too completely baffled to be disagreeable. Whatever it was he looked at Sherm and said, 'I never scuffed so much dust nor yanked out so much buck-brush'n weeds. Sherm . . . ?'

'I'll go over it for you again. The horse was staggerin' further on. The bank robber must've been pitched head-on into the tree. His face was cranked around with his chin over his shoulder. He was as dead as a person can get.'

'An' where was the saddle-bags?'

'I didn't see 'em, Travis.'

'Marshal, when that danged horse hit the tree it busted the cinch loose. Didn't you see the saddle lyin' there?'

'I saw . . . I didn't see the saddle-pockets.'

'Well now, boy, you was the first, the onliest person to get out there.'

Sherm sat a long time looking at the

older man before he eventually shoved upright, fed the last of the faggots into the fire and stood with his back to the older man watching flames nibble around the new wood.

He felt like he'd been yanked through a knothole: his head ached, his back hurt and his arms felt like lead. When he eventually turned, Will had entered the *jacal* and spoke. 'Pa, we need grub an' water, ten hours sleep and a creek to wash in. You want to set here, go right ahead. I'm goin' back.'

The older man stared at his son. 'Boy, that there's your inheritance, along with the ranch. It's out there some place. All right, you go back, but I want Sherm to stay here with me. We're goin' to find them saddle-pouches if we stay here until Christmas.'

Sherm flared up at the old man. 'You're a stubborn old bastard, Travis. I got no more to say about them bags'n you have an' I'm goin' back too.'

Travis was raising his face in the town marshal's direction when the old prospector appeared.

He walked up to Travis and dropped some scarred, dirty saddle-bags in front of him as he said, 'You better count it. I maybe made off with some of it.'

Travis ignored the speaker and his sarcasm as he reached for the bags and fumbled so badly with the hasps that Bernabe Swift sank to one knee, pushed Travis roughly aside, unbuckled the latches and flipped back the tongues.

Travis pulled the bags into his lap and dug into the nearest one. No one seemed to be breathing as he withdrew his gnarled, scarred fist. The greenbacks had been counted into bundles of a hundred dollars a bundle.

Travis kept digging. Bundles of greenbacks spilled from his lap. His son pushed up, picked up three bundles and shoved them back where they had come from and when his father raised a pair of glaring eyes, Will said, 'It'll keep, for Chris'sake. Let's get back, me'n my horse are starvin'. Sherm needs the medicine man . . . '

Will roughly rebuckled the pockets, caught his father by the arm and wrenched him up to his feet.

There were horses to spare. Will gave the surplus to Bernabe Swift along with a wad of paper money from a trouser pocket. The animals were tucked up like gutted snowbirds.

They went back the way they had come, Will Culley in the lead. Bernabe Swift hadn't told Travis where he'd found the saddle-bags.

Burros are the most inquisitive animals on earth. One of them had gotten his teeth into the saddle-bags and was on his way home dragging them when Bernabe saw the drag marks, guessed what had happened from the tracks, recovered the bags and returned with them. He would tell that story to his dying day, but never to anyone in Culleyville.

Bernabe had the weapons, the saddle riggings and later, when he got around to it, the graves he made in the abandoned, haunted old Mex town.

191

The part he knew nothing about concerned the painful ride back for the men who had recovered the bank's money and who had left the bank robbers behind.

They could have reached town sooner if their mounts hadn't been unable to move out of a shambling walk. They saw rooftops as the sun was slanting away.

At the livery barn where they expected to be greeted by the gossipy proprietor, they cared for their animals, pitched in twice as much feed as the liveryman would have done, generously scooped rolled barley using the coffee can in the barrel for that purpose and went up as far as the jailhouse by way of an empty boardwalk, went inside, sat down and looked at one another. Travis Culley said, 'The eatery's still doin' business. I'll stand a round of everythin' we can eat.' He stood up, started for the door and led the way through descending gloom.

The proprietor was alone, had in fact

been crossing to the roadway window to put his closed sign when he saw the men heading his way from the jail-house.

He barely made it behind the counter when the men led by old Travis Culley walked in.

The caféman couldn't have moved if his life had depended on it. The blood had dried stiff on filthy clothing. His last customers of the day hadn't washed or shaved and not a word was said until the hollow-eyed patrons were at the counter, than Travis Culley ordered.

'Whatever you got that's hot an' lots of it, an' the biggest pitcher of water you own. Do it fast, friend, we haven't eaten since I forgot.'

When the caféman disappeared behind the old army blanket that served as a door between his cooking area and his feeding trough where the most bedraggled, filthy, sunken-eyed men he had ever served sat hunched in a powerful silence, one man spoke in a gravelly voice.

'Anyone know where that banker lives? I'd like to roust him out an' empty these here saddle-bags in his lap.'

There was no response. The caféman appeared to fill mugs with black java. As he did this he said, 'Marshal. There's a pair of lawmen from down south come to town yestiddy mornin' wantin' to see you.'

Sherm nodded and tried to get comfortable on the unpadded bench which ran the length of the counter. The caféman said a trifle more. 'Feller who runs the waterin' — hole told me this marnin' when he come to breakfast those two are more'n likely unhappy that you wasn't in town.'

Will and his father exchanged a look but said nothing until the caféman went out of sight on the far side of the old army blanket, then the younger Culley said, 'I might just ride into the Red Rock country until they leave. Deming's more'n likely kept that bounty still on me.'

His father shook his head. 'You stay,

boy. In your old room. If they want you they got to find you.'

Travis might have said more but the platters heaped with food arrived.

Sherm nudged Will. 'I can lock you up again. No one can take you unless I let 'em, an' right now I'm not in a good mood for lettin' prisoners loose.'

Travis growled around a cud of corned beef. 'He comes home with me an' no matter if it's the army, he stays. Thanks all the same, Sherm.'

By the time the caféman's diners could hold no more and arose to leave, full night was down. If there was a moon it was not visible inside the eatery.

Normally the next stop would have been the saloon. Not this night. After a spell at the jailhouse, Travis and his son headed for the ranch in the Red Rock country, the marshal fought against a visit to Lisbeth Deane's cottage to see her brother. Instead he went up to the barber shop, got an annoyed proprietor to haul water for an all-over bath and relaxed in hot water until he twice fought off the urge to sleep, and eventually went to his room to bed down.

Not just yet.

He was ready to swing his feet and legs under the blankets when someone resoundingly put a gloved fist to his door and when that brought no immediate response, called in a bass-toned voice and announced himself. It was Emory Hubbard, Culleyville's physician and occasional surgeon.

How he had known the manhunters were back was anyone's guess, but Doctor Hubbard was a shockle-headed bear of a man, a hard drinker at times, an earthy practitioner who never faulted a diagnosis, a pregnancy, or, as it turned out, a bullet-grazed scalp. Nor had he come unprepared.

He got the marshal propped up in bed and asked questions as he worked. The only comment he made about Bernabe Swift's involvement was: 'A Rebel surgeon? No wonder they lost the war. Now hold still, this stuff burns.'

The whole story came out between growls and groans and when Doctor Hubbard was repacking his satchel he looked at Sherm and said, 'The other ones are dead?'

Sherm nodded. He was having difficulty keeping his eyes open.

The next thing he knew was that there was a dog fight in progress close by and the gummer who insisted on using a bugle to summon the volunteers when there was an emergency, was practising, again, and the sun was flooding past his window.

He felt better, not a lot better, a hungry better. At the eatery he was bombarded with questions and at least ten or twelve of Culleyville's townsmen cornered him for the details of all that had happened since he'd left town.

In clean clothes, shaved and shorn, wearing a smaller bandage he went to visit Al Burton. When Lisbeth opened the door one hand flew to her face the other hand to his sleeve as she said,

'Sherm! You should quit minding the law. Come along. Al's been worrying.'

Lisbeth left them alone and for the dozenth time Sherm was obliged to relate the story from beginning to the end.

10

They Come in All Sizes

Al Burton's injury was healing well, but for as long as Burton lived it would act as a reminder of his being in the right place at the wrong time.

Lisbeth brought hot coffee. Al scowled. He'd had his share of visitors of which all but one drank coffee. He told the marshal he had never liked coffee and he was beginning to transfer some of that dislike to his guests who drank the stuff.

He was peevish which Sherm thought he was entitled to be and he asked questions. The town marshal was unable to escape until the wounded man's sister came to the bedroom doorway to say there was a stranger outside asking to see the local lawman.

Sherm left the bedroom, met the

large man outside and invited him to walk to the jailhouse.

Up there Sherm dropped the *tranca* into its hangers, effectively barring the door from being opened, invited the large man to have a seat, which the large man did, and brought forth an impressive policeman's badge imprinted Deming New Mexico Police Department.

Sherm leaned back from his desk to say, 'You're a fair distance from home, mister.'

'Carl Wright, Marshal. I read some telegrams from up here.' Wright pushed out his legs, leaned to get comfortable and spoke again. 'It's about a coach bein' robbed an' the whip gettin' shot.'

Sherm gravely inclined his head. He hadn't thought anyone from New Mexico could be in Culleyville for any other reason, so he launched into a recital beginning with the other New Mexicans arriving in town and ending with the shootout in the abandoned Mex town south-east of Culleyville.

The man from Deming wanted to know if money had been recovered.

Sherm answered that question too and added the origin of the $31,000.

'You brought it back?' the large man said, and Sherm nodded. 'To the last dime far as I know. About the renegades, we left 'em in that Mex village, dead.'

'All three of 'em?'

Sherm's gaze narrowed a fraction. He had not mentioned how many men from New Mexico had been at the Mex village. He leaned forward with hands clasped atop his desk. 'Only names I heard was Holding, Tex something or other, and Carter. Walt Carter.'

'All dead, Marshal?'

'That's what I said. Mister Wright, I'd be almighty interested in why you're up here.'

The bear-built man went to work creating a quirly and did not speak until it was lighted. Then he said, 'There was four. The one you didn't put a name to went south, down into ol' Messico by

201

our calculations, an' he wasn't important if we never find him.'

Wright deeply inhaled and exhaled. 'It's the other three. Tell me, Marshal, did you search 'em after the fight?'

'If you mean did we find any money, the answer is we got back the thirty-one thousand, left 'em where they fell an' come home. The money we recovered was the same amount as was stolen from our bank.' Sherm twisted to point in a corner where he'd last seen the saddle-bags. They were not there.

He faced forward and exchanged a long look with the Deming city policeman who said, 'Not there, Marshal?'

Sherm nodded his head.

'Who could've got in here last night to make off with it?'

Sherm was too shocked to answer. He shook his head, arose, went to the corner where the leather pockets had been left and gently wagged his head before facing around. 'No one, Mr Wright. There's never been anyone break in here an' to my knowledge no more'n three broke out.'

Wright considered the top of his cigarette before saying, 'Someone did, Marshal, sure as hell someone did.' Wright stood up. He was massively impressive sitting or standing. He showed a wintry smile. 'I'll help you find it, Marshal, but it's really none of my concern. You plumb certain those highbinders was all dead?'

'I'm more'n sure.'

'About that old Johnny Reb you mentioned?'

'Bernabe Swift?'

'Yes, him.'

'No, sir, Travis counted the money an' far as I know it was all there. He'd have bellered like a bloody-hand In'ian if it hadn't all been there. Mostly it was his money.'

The lawman from Deming made a reasonable statement. 'Then it was him. I don't see how it could — '

The policeman cut himself off in mid-sentence; they stood looking at each other until Sherm said, 'It don't make sense.' The more massive and older lawman made a taciturn rebuttal. 'It always makes sense, Marshal, when money ups and disappears. I got to use your telegraph office.'

After Carl Wright left Sherm sat down at his desk . . . and fell asleep.

He did not awaken until the large New Mexican came in out of the hot afternoon and acted as though nothing was out of the ordinary.

He went to the wall bench, dropped down and concentrated on building a quirly, acting as though he hadn't noticed that Sherm had been napping. When Sherm shifted on his chair, yawned and shook his head, the New Mexican said, 'Something I got to tell you, Marshal. There's a feller up here named Will Culley who was tied in with that coach robbery down south. You know him?'

Sherm softly sighed and answered. 'I know him. I had him locked up. He's the feller was at the gunfight when we got back the money. Why?'

'Well, Marshal, that feller who run for it toward Messico, they caught him. I got a telegraph last night. He said Will Culley got some of the stage loot. Marshal, I asked around; folks told me where I most likely could find Culley. I was wonderin' if you'd like to ride along. I don't know my way around up here.'

Sherm leaned and clasped his hands. 'Mister, Will didn't have any of that stage loot. I'll bet my life on it. You mentioned Walt Carter . . . '

'You said he got shot, Marshal?'

'Mister Wright, I'll tell you what I figure; you're not goin' to like it.'

'Most likely not. What is it?'

'The lawmen where you came from got that money, divvied it up, an' if you didn't know anythin' about this, then I got to guess someone down there sent you up here to get rid of you.'

The large man arose ponderously, stubbed out his smoke and faced Sherm across the desk without speaking for a full sixty seconds then he said, 'Son of a bitch! They give me a hunnert dollars for expenses. Marshal, until this minute it never came to me.' The large man returned to his bench, dropped down gazing steadily at the town marshal. 'I tracked 'em. I caught the feller who fled down into Messico . . . son of a bitch! He told me pretty much the same thing an' he showed me what was left of what he swore was his share.'

Sherm eased back off the desk and for a while slumped gazing at his guest before saying, 'Who do you want to believe?'

The large man did not immediately respond, but eventually he said, 'You reckon Will Culley could verify any of this?'

Sherm shrugged. 'I don't know.' He had an errant thought. 'The driver of that stage is staying here with his sister. You want to talk to him?'

The big man pondered and eventually shook his head. 'He didn't have a part in the robbery, near as I know.'

Sherm agreed without saying so. He made another suggestion. 'All right, I'll ride out to the Culley place with you, but I got to tell you Will's pa has a real short fuse.'

'How long'll it take us out an' back?'

'What's left of the day.'

Carl Wright did not look enthusiastic, but he reset his hat and went as far as the door where he waited.

Down at the livery barn, the proprietor sized up the stranger before leading up a 1,200 pound animal and went about rigging him for riding. Sherm had the answer about how the big man had arrived in town — by stagecoach.

While they were travelling westerly from town, Sherm went into considerable detail about the Culleys, old Travis and young Will his son. He also related the story of the gunfight at that empty Mex hamlet and when he finished and they had rooftops in sight, Carl Wright turned a solemn face and asked a question. 'About them big red rocks over yonder: you don't suppose young Culley cached anything over there do you?'

Sherm's reply was dour. 'I don't expect so. I keep tellin' you he wasn't in on what really happened after AI Burton got shot an' Will come back here. Neither of 'em . . . it was the local law down in Deming. I'd guess they planned this an' waited for a bullion stage to come along so's they could make it work . . . an' you friend, you'd likely know why they wanted you out of the country down there.'

Carl Wright was studying the buildings when he said, 'In Deming there's hell to pay over losin' that money. It was gone, so was the highwaymen.'

Sherm took it up. 'An' they got rid of you too, the same way. They sent you up here believin' that cock an' bull story.'

The large man was passing beyond the gate into the yard when he said, 'Marshal, if you're right when I get back down there somebody's goin' to wish I was never born.'

Travis was on the porch watching as his Mexican went to take care of horses. Sherm led off toward the porch where he introduced Carl Wright, and Travis, barring access to his chair, shook hands and sat down.

Carl Wright had no reason to be tactful nor was he. He wanted to know where Travis's son was and got a short answer. 'He's out lookin' for heifers in trouble. It's that time of the year, Mr Wright.'

The big man nodded which settled in Sherm's mind as well as in the mind of Travis that Carl Wright either was or had been associated with cattle.

Sherm hitched up his haunch and perched on the porch's peeled-log railing. Carl Wright remained standing. He told old Travis who he was and why he was in the Culleyville country.

Travis digested all this, flicked a look at the town marshal and said, 'Sherm told you about them other fellers up here from Deming?'

Wright nodded. 'He told me. They was up here to find the money too.'

Travis put a narrow-eyed look on the large man. 'You, too, friend; you believe the money's up here?'

'Well, mostly I don't think so but I wanted to hear your son's version.'

'All he knows, Mr Wright, is that he helped stop the coach. He didn't know it was carryin' money.' Travis hunched a little in his rocker. 'You care for a shot of brightener, Mr Wright?'

The large man surprised Sherm. He smiled at Travis and nodded. As the old man went inside Sherm said, 'Be careful. I think he makes his own corn squeezin's.'

Travis returned with three cups, handed two of them around, got back in his chair and hoisted his glass. They drank without a toast after which Travis said, 'Mister Wright, I'd say you bein' a Texan an' all . . . '

Wright held out his empty cup and did as he'd done before, he smiled without speaking.

Travis returned. Sherm took his cup and put it aside. Carl Wright and Travis downed their jolts and the large man said, 'That's a mighty fine chair, Mr Culley. Did you make it?'

Travis stood up. His eyes were bright. 'Set in it, Mr Wright. Yessir, I made it. Go ahead'n rock.'

The large man rocked and Travis reclaimed his tin cup and went back inside.

Sherm eyed the large man. He fitted the rocking chair like he'd used a shoe horn to get into it.

Travis returned with two cups. He ignored the town marshal. Sherm saw Felice peering around from behind the barn.

Carl Wright sat and rocked and smiled. He said, 'It's a sight better ridin' this chair than any horse I ever set on.'

Travis nodded without agreeing or disagreeing. He glared at Sherm who told the large man they'd ought to be heading back and Carl Wright pushed

211

up out of the chair. Travis went to stand by it.

'Sherm,' he said. 'You'n Mr Wright come back any time you're in the country.' Travis faced the larger man with an outstretched hand. 'Mister Wright, it was a pure pleasure. You come back, you hear?'

Wright gave Travis a friendly pat on the shoulder. 'When your boy comes in,' he said, 'tell him I was here an' if he's ever down in my country to look me up.'

Travis said, 'Wait a minute, gents,' and returned to the house. When he returned he had two cups. He and Carl Wright saluted each other, swallowed once and the big man followed Sherm. He had a little difficulty mounting his livery horse. Felice helped.

In the saddle, Wright took his time evening up the reins after which he followed Sherm in the direction of town. When they were halfway the big man wiped his eyes on a blue bandanna and said, 'You said he had a short fuse,

Marshal. He's as hospitable a gent as I've ever met . . . is he from Texas?'

'Years back, Mr Wright. About forty years back. Why?'

'He's got Texas manners. Folks in my country is born with manners, hospitality and fine manners. You can tell us a mile off by our way of bein' decent.'

They entered the livery barn from the west-side alley and the liveryman met them in the runway. He watched Wright fumble with the latigo, shot a look at Sherm, who shrugged.

The liveryman ended up off-rigging the big studnecked mare. As he was doing this he dropped a clanger. 'Will's in town. I figured all you fellers went through he wouldn't make the ride for a week.'

When Sherm glanced around, Carl Wright was looking at him. Wright said, 'Will? Does he mean Travis's boy?'

The liveryman spoke before the marshal could. 'Yes. Will Culley. Folks say he's sweet on Al Burnton's sister.'

Wright asked if Sherm knew where

Will could be found and with the liveryman standing there he said, 'I know, but Burton's bad off from gettin' shot durin' that hold-up down in your country.'

'Burton?'

'He was the whip. Didn't they tell you down yonder the whip got shot?'

'They didn't mention the driver, just mostly talked about the highwaymen an' that they was up here most likely with the stolen money.'

Sherm shook his head. The men in Deming knew the whip had been shot. He thought it most likely just about everyone down there would know that. He looked steadily at Carl Wright and the big man was scowling when he spoke.

'They was in such a gawddamned hurry to get me headin' up here. I wondered while I was comin'. Now I think I understand a couple of things . . . those galled sons of bitches!'

Sherm led the way to Lisbeth Deane's cottage and got a surprise, Dr

Hubbard was in with Al. Lisbeth took the visitors to her brother's bedroom. Doc Hubbard was working with rolled-up sleeves and a basin of water. He looked around once, growled a greeting, slowly began wiping his hands as he turned more slowly, and spoke. 'Bud . . . ?'

Carl Wright widely smiled. 'Emory?'

The two men gripped outstretched hands. The doctor saw only the large man. He said, 'Bud? What in hell are you doin' in this place?'

'Followin' you, Emory. That settler you stole the horse from a few years back . . . '

'Few years,' exclaimed the medicine man. 'Fifteen, eighteen years back . . . Bud?'

'I got a place down near Deming. Got talked into leavin' to come up here an' find whoever stopped a stage an' made off with some money.'

Doctor Hubbard gestured for the benefit of the other people in the room. 'Bud an' I were in the army together years back.'

Al Burton, half bare in the bed said, 'Doc, finish this damned bandaging!'

Carl Wright gazed at the irate man in the bed. 'Who shot you?' he asked, and got a tart answer.

'Some bastards who couldn't shoot a hole in a barn from the inside . . . *Doc!*'

As the medical practitioner moved back toward the bed the big man eyed the only chair in the room and started toward it. He staggered six feet from his objective and Lisbeth squealed.

Sherm helped Wright onto the chair and held him until he was sure the big man was all right. Sherm said, 'We was out at Travisys. Him an' Travis threw 'em off like they was water. Where's Will? Mister Wright's here about that damned stage robbery down in the Deming country. He wants to hear Will's story. I thought Will'd be here.'

Lisbeth blushed, as her brother said, 'He was here a while back. Him an' my sister billed an' cooed in the kitchen.

He might still be in town.' Burton glanced at his sister. 'Didn't Will say he had to see the banker?'

Lisbeth nodded and left the bedroom. As Doc Hubbard returned to the bedside he and the large New Mexican continued to reminisce until Sherm said he'd go look for Will, Wright could meet him at the jailhouse when he was ready.

Sherm paused outside the house. He could see both sides of the road northward. There were a few pedestrians but young Culley was not among them.

He headed for the bank and almost made it, someone hailed him from across the road. Sherm veered off, was halfway toward the saloon when the harness-maker collared him. Sherm swore under his breath, reversed course and met the harness-maker in front of the leather works.

The harness-maker was fumbling in back to untie his apron when he said, 'If you're lookin' for Travis's boy he was at the bank an' stopped in the shop with me for a spell then went to get his horse.'

As this was being said, Will came from the lower end of town astride a Roman-nosed buckskin horse. Sherm hailed him from the plankwalk. Will reined over and swung off.

Sherm said, 'While you was in the Deming country did you know a big feller named Carl Wright?'

Will shook his head. 'I didn't know him but I know who he was. Has a big cow outfit down there. Was county sheriff years back. Why, Sherm?'

'Your pappy got him so drunk he couldn't find the floor with both hands. I rode out there with him. He wants to talk to you.'

Will leaned and tipped his head before saying, 'It'll have to be a short confab. I want to be home about supper-time. Where is he?'

'Down at Lisbeth's house. Him an' the medicine man soldiered together years back.'

Will looked annoyed. 'If you don't tell him we met . . . I got to get home . . . I returned the bank's money . . . been lookin' for you to tell you. I'll be out there if he wants to ride out.'

Young Culley went to his horse, swung astride and looked at the marshal. 'Pa got him drunk?'

'Will, it come on to him all of a sudden. He dang near passed out in Al Burton's bedroom.'

Will laughed as he reined clear and boosted his animal into a mile-eating lope.

11

A Hunch

Sherm was at the café when the large man from Deming walked in, sat at the counter near Sherm and said, 'Where's the caféman?'

'In the kitchen; he'll be along.'

'All I want is black coffee an' plenty of it.'

Sherm grinned. 'I warned you about old Travis.'

The caféman appeared, filled three cups with coffee and placed them in front of Carl Wright. 'Anything else?' he asked.

Wright shook his head while reaching for the first cup. Sherm told him Will would be at the ranch if he wanted to ride out there again, and got a murderous look. 'You want to come with me? This time if that old man comes at me with whiskey I'm goin' to straddle him an' pour it down him.'

Sherm said, 'First thing in the morning,' watched Carl Wright reach for the third cup, spilled silver beside his empty plate and walked out into a cool evening.

He was satisfied he had it all figured out. He would have liked it better if the renegade police down in Deming would have sent the highwaymen in some other direction.

He was at the rooming-house when the local blacksmith hammered the door and when Sherm opened it the blacksmith held out something. 'Give this to Travis next time you see him. I got no reason to ride out there for as far ahead as I can see. Besides, I don't like that old goat.'

The blacksmith turned back the way he had come leaving the town marshal holding something heavy in his hand.

He closed the door, took the object where lamplight showed and stared.

It was a stirrup. Sherm had seen

hundreds of stirrups in his time but never one as heavy as this one was. He turned it over twice, hefted it and placed it on his room's chair where he wouldn't forget it in the morning.

He fell asleep, puzzling about the stirrup. If he'd been asked he would have said the stirrup was solid iron.

Mexicans used metal stirrups, usually they were covered with sewn and engraved leather. He'd been told as a youngster no one in their right mind rode a saddle with metal stirrups, if an animal fell he would likely bend the metal around a man's foot which was a good way to get dragged to death.

He was awakened before sunrise by a rooster welcoming the new day. It was dark, but by the time he cleaned up out back at the wash-house and got dressed, daylight had arrived.

He headed for the café, the proprietor's first customer. By the time he had finished breakfast several other patrons had arrived.

He went down to the livery barn and

got a genuine surprise, Carl Wright was sitting comfortably on a wall bench inside the runway. Sherm would have bet the price of a new hat the big man would be hung-over. He wasn't. At least the way he greeted the town marshal gave no indication Wright might have a headache.

They saddled up in silence. The liveryman did not arrive until they were leading their horses outside to be mounted.

It was chilly. There would be no appreciable amount of warmth in the new day until about the time they reached the Culley place.

Wright eyed the stirrup Sherm had secured behind his cantle by a skirting thong.

Sherm passed it over. The big man was as intrigued as Sherm had been the previous evening. He asked if Sherm had a mate and got a negative answer. Wright then wanted to know where Sherm had gotten the stirrup and this time the answer posed more questions.

'All I know is that the blacksmith brought it to me last night to give to Travis Culley.'

The big man returned the stirrup and rode in silence until they had the ranch buildings in sight, then Sherm looked at the man riding stirrup with him. 'You knock back more of Travis's brew an' I'll leave you where you fall.'

Wright growled a response as Felice appeared out of nowhere which seemed to be his custom and was waiting to take their horses.

Travis wasn't on the porch. Felice said he and Will had gone bull hunting over where those red rocks had both water and graze.

Felice did not know when the Culleys would return but made a guess. 'Supper-time. *El viejo* don't like missing supper.'

Sherm led the way to the porch. His companion settled into the rocking chair, gazed far out and talked of cattle, land, water, the things stockmen generally talked about sooner or later.

Felice came over to say there were two riders coming, and used his raised right hand.

Sherm had the heavy stirrup at his feet when Felice said, 'You found it?'

Sherm considered the mahogany-coloured features of Obregon. 'This stirrup? Was it lost?'

'Well, one that looked just like it. Is it heavy?'

Sherm handed the stirrup to Felice who briefly hefted and smilingly returned it. 'As heavy,' he said, and started to leave the porch to be available when Travis and his son rode in. Sherm stopped him.

'Where is the other stirrup?'

Felice shrugged. 'In the house, maybe . . . I don't know. I only saw it once, when Will came home the first time.'

Carl Wright's interest was aroused. 'You sure it was a mate to this one?'

Felice was hiking toward the yard where the riders would arrive. He either did not hear the big man or regarded his obligation to care for the Culley horses as more important. Sherm placed the stirrup behind Travis's rocker and Carl Wright frowned. 'He'll see it.'

Sherm agreed. 'I expect he will.'

The father and son met Felice who told them who was waiting on the porch before leading the animals away to be cuffed, watered and fed.

Will called from the corral and Sherm raised an arm in acknowledgement. Carl Wright arose from the rocker and extended a hand without smiling. 'That's almighty home whiskey you make, Mr Culley.'

Travis eyed the larger man. 'You liked to emptied a bottle, Mr Wright. Care for me to open another one?'

'No thanks,' Wright replied and stooped to pick up the heavy iron stirrup.

Both the Culleys seemed turned to stone. Travis held out his hand. When Wright handed the stirrup over Will let go with an audible sigh before saying, 'Where did it come from?'

Sherm explained, and Will took the stirrup from his father, hefted it a couple of times and looked at his father. 'Where would he have got it?'

The older man perched on the peeled-log porch railing clearly lost in thought. He heard what Sherm said but seemed not to have heard as Will moved toward the door holding the iron stirrup in one hand.

His father said, 'With the other one, boy,' and waited until his son had disappeared inside before addressing his visitors.

'It's a sort of keepsake. Me'n Will figured to find it in them red rocks.'

Sherm tilted his hat brim down to avoid sunlight. 'Mind telling me . . . is there some kind of story connected with it, Travis?'

'Well, not exactly . . . I got to find out how that damned blacksmith come to have it.'

Will returned to the porch. Sherm thought his face was slightly flushed but said nothing.

Travis said, 'Match, Will?'

'Like two peas in a pod.'

Carl Wright sat down and rocked a little. 'Mister Culley, that's the first iron stirrup I've ever seen. I've heard of Messicans usin' them. There's stories of a horse fallin' an' its rider getting drug to his death when the horse jumped up an' ran.'

Travis nodded. He'd heard those old tales. Travis clearly wanted the visitors to leave. Will sat on the porch floor. He too seemed preoccupied. Sherm glanced at Carl Wright and gave his head a slight sideways nod.

Wright did not move. When the silence had drawn out enough to be uncomfortable Carl Wright addressed Travis. 'That stirrup had kind of got my curiosity up, Mr Culley.'

Travis perched on the peeled-log railing and almost smiled. 'Nothin' that would interest a stranger, Mr Wright. They belonged to Will's mother.'

'She rode iron stirrups on her saddle?'

Travis shifted on the railing. 'Women do odd things, Mr Wright. She also used to go prospectin' among them red rocks. Just before she got taken down sick she come back carryin' them two heavy stirrups. Later when her'n I was ridin' over there she showed me the place where she found 'em. A real narrow, real tall crevice. Gents, if you figure to get back to town before the caféman locks up for the day . . . ' Travis stood clear of the railing and his son left the porch in the direction of the barn.

Sherm nodded at Carl Wright. The two of them thanked Travis for his hospitality, the common thing to do, and walked in the direction of the barn where Felice had one horse saddled and was working on the other one. Wright spoke aside to Sherm. 'Somethin' don't smell right.'

Sherm agreed, led his horse outside to be mounted and there was no sign of the Culleys on the porch.

Sherm was quiet after they left the

yard. Wright's attempts to get a conversation going failed completely. Twice Sherm twisted to look back. All he saw both times was an immensity of land with no movement.

He finally hauled to a dead stop and said, 'Mister Wright, you know the way to town from here?'

The large man nodded. 'You got somethin' in mind?'

'Well, I've known the Culleys since I came here. I never had 'em act the way they did back yonder today.'

Wright let his reins sag as he also scanned the countryside in the red-rock area. 'It was that stirrup. When the old man saw it, handled it, he was different.'

Sherm made a humourless smile, 'If you don't mind I'll leave you, go back an' do some snoopin'.'

The big man sagged in the saddle and regarded Sherm from beneath a tipped-forward hat brim. 'Two men are better'n one, Marshal.'

'Mister Wright, I got no right to go

230

back. Neither the old man or Will broke any law that I know of. In my job I got a right — sort of — to poke in the business of other folks. But you . . . '

Wright slowly evened up his reins, did not look at the town marshal as he did this, and quietly said, 'All right, but when I get back to town I'm goin' to find that blacksmith.'

Sherm nodded. 'His name's Grat Riordan. I'd admire to know how he come by that iron stirrup.'

Wright brusquely nodded and gigged his big lively animal in the direction of town.

Sherm watched him, was satisfied he would not turn back, reined northward and rode without haste until he had the red rocks on his left a mile or more westerly. This time he looked back in the direction of the Culley yard, house and barn. He was not sure what he expected to see and until his angling course took him closer to the red-rock country he saw nothing. He drew rein in the shade of an ancient gnarled tree emblazoned with indecipherable symbols so old the bark had nearly grown completely over them, then he saw them with the sun on their left leaving tracks in the direction of that place where he had met Travis while leading a horse.

He was reasonably safe from detection as long as he did not leave tree shade. The pair of riders would note movement.

He dismounted. His horse had picked up movement too and kept his head raised as he watched.

Sherm said, 'Son of a bitch!' and his horse completely ignored him in favour of the distant horsemen.

They boosted over into a lope. Sherm wasn't surprised. This day was beginning to head along toward sundown.

When a spur of immense boulders hid the two riders Sherm swung astride, closed the distance westerly until he was within the boulder field, then rode slowly to make an interception.

He was satisfied the riders were the

Culleys. Intuition told him they had a destination so he eventually dismounted and led his animal. He told his horse they were playing the childhood game of hide and seek.

The Culleys got into the field of prehistoric plinths somewhere southwesterly, possibly by that trail Sherm had used a few days before.

The difficulty was simply that if he found them before they knew he also was among the rocks he was going to have some explaining to do and for the life of him he could not think of what he would say.

He eventually reached the place where Travis had been scouted up by that large bird. Obviously at one time there had been a pond covering a few yards. Now the ground was as hard as iron without any vestige of water.

He got among some tall, more or less upright big rocks, dropped flat down and pressed an ear to the ground. In this very ancient, very soundless place the reverberations were barely audible.

A pair of horses was approaching from the south.

Sherm stood up, brushed off and sought a place of concealment of which there were many — for a man — not for his horse.

He started back the way he had come, leading the horse and pausing occasionally to listen. He detected nothing not even when he got belly down. The last time he did this he saw his own tracks in the million-year-old dust.

His heart sank. The Culleys would see the tracks, the only fresh tracks.

He selected a passageway between huge monoliths on his left, which was to the right and led off up through there, still on foot leading his animal.

What would happen when the Culleys saw his sign was either turn back, or possibly track him until sundown obscured his imprints.

He left the horse in one of those accidental cul-de-sacs Mother Nature habitually created and climbed the least tall side of his natural dog trot.

It was a long wait and when he caught movement it was of one horseman not two, and that was worrisome. The Culleys assuredly knew this ancient and undisturbed field of gigantic rocks. Being the hunted instead of the hunter changed everything.

Getting back to the horse required more crawling to avoid being skylined, than descending upright, the way he had got to his vantage point.

There was no way of determining whether Will and his father were tracking him. He led the horse further northward until the narrow runway widened.

On the east side of the passageway, a fair distance up, the huge red rock was what Sherm thought was a cave. Except that someone had hammered out a set of crude steps reaching almost to the dark slit. Sherm would have been more interested in what lay ahead, a wide opening completely surrounded by a placement of fortress-like rocks, not as tall as others but so thickly spaced that they formed a meadow-like circular area of about two or three acres.

Sherm led the horse to the debouchment beyond which was the grazed-over small meadow.

He stopped so abruptly the horse threw up its head to avoid a collision.

Near a southerly slit in the red-rock enclosure a man sat motionless on a bay horse. His back was to Sherm who tried to make his horse step backward far enough for them both to be concealed.

The horse backed as any broke cow horse knew to do.

Sherm looped his reins around a protruding scrub brush and returned to the point of vantage where he could see the meadow.

The horseman was not there, but a thin spindrift of ancient dust showed where he had exited the little meadow the way he had entered, through that passageway where Sherm had first seen him.

He listened, heard nothing and leaned against rough rocks pondering. If that horseman had been Will or his father, they were further into the rock field than Sherm thought they should have been — except for the clear possibility that at least one of them knew the area sufficiently well to cover distances by natural short cuts.

He went back to the horse, turned it and started back the way he had come.

It only occurred to him that he had been trapped when a horse nickered up ahead, down where Sherm had noticed the runway and had entered it.

He was slightly more than mid-way in his retreat when he heard the horse and stopped stone still, one hand resting on the nostrils of his own horse to prevent it answering.

It was hot in the passageway with no air stirring. He mopped off sweat, left the horse and crept carefully until he could see the open country where he had entered. There was nothing to be seen or heard.

Whoever was out there was one side or the other side from the exit.

He looked back. His horse impaired the sighting in that direction.

He leaned in a minimum of shade, mopped off more sweat and slumped. He was trapped. They had dogged his tracks to the place where they separated. Knowing this territory as they had to know it made it possible for them to surmise about where he had to be.

If there was a way to avoid being caught he could not imagine it. As for being caught — in open range country he had every right to be where he was, but walking out to be faced by either Travis or Will Culley would be embarrassing.

He retrieved the horse and started walking. At the narrow place where he had entered he saw no one. Not until he was clear of huge boulders, then he saw Travis grinning like a tame ape. Travis let the hand holding his six-gun droop. 'Marshal,' he said in a patronizing tone of voice. 'I sure didn't expect it would be you.'

Sherm's exasperation, tinged with the humiliation of being caught snooping, made his reply brusque.

'Was I gettin' close, Travis?'

Instead of giving an immediate reply the older man put two fingers in his mouth and whistled. The sound was shrill enough to achieve its purpose.

Will arrived using the same narrow passageway Sherm had used.

He dismounted, looked quizzically at his father and spoke. 'Close, Pa?'

Travis nodded without looking away from the marshal. He holstered his six-gun and let go a long sigh. 'Sherm, you cut back? Where's the big feller?'

'Ought to be close to town by now.'

'You're alone?'

Sherm was momentarily distracted when a horse fly tried to land on the nose of his saddle animal. After he'd routed the fly before it made its stinging bite he said, 'It came to me after we left your porch. There'd be a reason for you to get rid of me'n Mr Wright the way you did.'

Will spoke calmly, without rancour. 'Why here, Sherm? Pa's been keepin' folks out of the rocks. You'd know that. Why'd you come snooping? We ain't broke no law an' folks got the right to chase off trespassers.'

Sherm looked at the younger Culley. 'I don't know, Will. I just got a powerful urge, sort of a hunch.'

Travis wagged his head. 'Sherm, get on that horse an' don't even look back. An' one more thing: don't never come snoopin' around on our property, an' that includes the red rock territory.'

Sherm let the older man get it all said before speaking. 'Travis, we've been neighbourly a long time. I wasn't snoopin'.'

'That's what I call it, Sherm. Get on your horse an' remember, don't you ever come back in here, never. Now git!'

Will was eyeing his father. His own expression was not flushed with anger.

240

In fact, as Sherm snugged up the cinch before mounting, Will said, 'Pa!'

The old man flared. 'Boy, we mind our own business an' expect others to do the same. Marshal, git!'

Sherm regarded Will a long moment from the saddle before nodding. He only barely glanced at the older Culley as he readied his reins, nor did he look at Travis when he said, 'You can't expect a man to just close off his curiosity, Travis. Folks aren't made that way.'

The older man's six-gun seemed to jump into Travis's hand. 'Never, Sherm. Never as long as you live ever come back here. The red-rock country is out of bounds for you, as long as you live. You let me catch you bein' curious again an' I'll bury you in here. *Git!*'

As Sherm hugged his horse with both knees he did not look at either of the Culleys. He worked his way clear of the monstrous rocks, twice took the wrong path and by the time he got clear, with the red-rock country behind him, he twisted to look back.

There was no sign of the Culleys.

It was a respectable distance to town and he did not hasten. A hunch inclined him to believe he had been close to whatever old Travis got so upset about.

As for never returning, he leaned to expectorate to one side and watched Culleyville's evening lights come out to him.

He was intercepted by Carl Wright at a piddling spring where the large man had evidently planned his ambush, reined, waited until Carl Wright was close then drily said, 'I got caught.'

Wright wasn't surprised. 'I turned back after a mile or so. There was no sign of you but those two Culleys was ridin' hell for leather toward them red rocks . . . I almost went back.'

'Why didn't you, Mr Wright?'

'Because I figured they'd see me comin' and that'd spoil whatever you was up to . . . you hungry?'

Sherm did not answer, he rattled his

242

reins and as the horse resumed its way toward town Carl Wright fell in beside Sherm and neither of them spoke until they were crossing the west-side alley toward the livery barn. Then Carl Wright said, 'That old man's got some sort of secret an' I'm not convinced it don't have somethin' to do with that missin' stage money from down in the Deming country.'

Sherm was too disgusted to answer, he swung off, led his animal inside and handed the reins to the liveryman.

Wright did the same. As Sherm left the barn heading for his office Carl Wright followed about halfway then veered off, crossed to the far plankwalk and went up to the saloon.

Sherm lighted his jailhouse hanging lamp, dumped his hat on the table, groped in a lower desk drawer for his mostly empty bottle, took it to the little barred roadway window and took two thoughtful pulls before blowing out a flammable breath and returning the bottle to its dark place and locking up his jailhouse and walking in the direction of the café. The proprietor saw him coming, groaned and did not put the Closed sign in his roadway window.

12

Visitin' Around

A man is likely to sleep on a full gut. Sherm Kandelin was at the eatery the following morning in a morose mood, largely unnoticed by the mob of other breakfasting men whose banter was loud and wide ranging. After a couple of efforts to get the town marshal involved in the conversation, the other diners ignored him, until the old recluse who owned the boarding-house came in, got beside the lawman, leaned and whispered, then departed without so much as a 'good mornin' to the other diners.

Sherm straightened on the counter bench, emptied his coffee cup in two swallows, put coins beside his empty plate and left the café. As soon as he was gone, one of the remaining diners said, 'Somethin' goin' on sure as hell. That old scarecrow never leaves his hotel not even for breakfast.'

The speculation was wide ranging without including the caféman who was as busy as a kitten in a box of sand feeding his customers before any delay would bring their tirade down on him.

Sherm went to the jailhouse, nodded to Lisbeth Deane who was sitting on the wall bench twisting and untwisting a scrap of a lace handkerchief in her fingers. Sherm inaugurated the conversation with an incorrect guess. 'Al's not doin' well, Lisbeth?'

'Al's coming right along. In all of our life together, I've never seen him as cranky as he is now. Marshal, do you know Grat Riordan?'

Sherm leaned forward on the desk top. 'Everyone knows Grat, Lisbeth. He's the only worthwhile horse-shoer in the countryside. Why? He did somethin'?'

'No. I . . . he's a hard man to like, but

him an' my brother have been friends for ages. Al always said Grat was a man you could trust.'

Sherm nodded. Like other folks around Culleyville he did not especially like the blacksmith who was an unsmiling, unfriendly individual but an excellent metalworker. 'He bothered your brother, Lisbeth?'

'No . . . I'd best start at the beginning. You remember Will Culley's mother?'

'Yes'm. We wasn't close, but I remember her, an' I remember how you'n her was close. I figured you was the daughter she never had from the way she'd come to town in the top buggy an' visit with you for hours. I never heard a bad word about her, Lisbeth.'

'Sherm, a while before she was taken to her death bed she brought some real nice cloth for me'n her to make dresses out of.'

Sherm nodded; instead of getting closer for Lisbeth Deane to get to the point of her visit she seemed to Sherm to be getting further from it. He leaned back off the desk.

'Like you said, Sherm, we were close. Like a mother an' a daughter.'

Sherm nodded and cleared his throat. He had no trouble believing that kind of a relationship had existed. Old Travis's wife rarely came to town and when she did . . .

'Sherm, the last time she came visiting she gave me somethin' to hide for her.'

He nodded again. 'An' you hid it . . . Lisbeth?'

'Yes; an' I figured someday I'd hire a rig an' take it an' give it to Travis. He was her rightful heir.'

'What did you do with it, Lisbeth?'

'Day before yesterday when Grat was playin' checkers with Al in his bedroom I asked if he'd do me a favour. He said he'd be proud to so I got the old stirrup gave it to him to give to you because folks know you've been goin' out to the Culley place real often lately. Did he give you a big heavy old stirrup, Sherm?'

The marshal nodded his head. 'He gave it to me an' I gave it to Travis. Lisbeth, what did she tell you about the stirrup?'

'Sherm, there was times when she'd get lonely.'

The marshal nodded. He had no difficulty believing that. Being married to Travis Culley would be no bed of roses.

'She'd visit with me sometimes all morning. We'd talk and work on the dresses and visit a lot. Times when she couldn't come to town she'd explore those big red rocks. You know the ones? About a mile or so from the Culley yard.'

Sherm nodded as he crisply said, 'I know 'em, Lisbeth.'

'That's where she found it. In a cave part-way up one of those red-rock hills. There was a skeleton in there partly covered with some kind of armour. She said she thought he'd been one of those

Spaniards who came into the country long ago. She brought back one stirrup an' gave it to her husband after she painted it black.'

Sherm nodded again. The stirrup had been covered thickly with black paint.

'What'd she do with the other stirrup?'

Lisbeth looked blankly at the marshal. 'She never mentioned another stirrup to her husband. She also painted it black and gave it to me to give her husband after she died.'

Sherm frowned. 'Why would she do that? Why not give him both stirrups?'

'Because after she gave him the first one she told me he changed overnight. He took the stirrup up to Cheyenne and sold it to a money man.'

Sherm's frown turned into a deep frown of bafflement. Lisbeth had both hands lying in her lap like a small dead bird. 'Those stirrups were made of solid gold. Her husband was different with all that money. She didn't want to have to go through that again, but she loved him, she wanted him to have the second stirrup but not until she was gone.'

'Did she . . . was she real sick, Lisbeth?'

'She was dying. Two doctors up north told her she'd last maybe a year.'

Sherm resettled in his chair and leaned back looking at Lisbeth without blinking.

She arose from the bench. 'Mister Culley now has the second stirrup?'

Sherm answered as he, too, stood up. 'He has . . . Lisbeth, he acted . . . different when I gave it to him. That cave where she found the stirrups, did she find anything else?'

'Not that she told me about. She couldn't understand why someone would make a pair of stirrups out of pure gold.'

Sherm agreed, it didn't make sense to him either, but later, much later, he would imagine at least a dozen reasons why someone would do it. Also later, much later, he was convinced that he nor anyone else would ever know why it had been done.

He visited the smithy. The story the blacksmith related was exactly as Lisbeth Deane had passed it on to him.

Later in the day, between midday and dusk, he was dining at the eatery when the large man from Deming walked in, lightly tapped Sherm's shoulder and sat beside him at the counter. He ordered, put a long look on the coffee pot dead ahead and said, 'I been thinking.'

Sherm had too. 'You come up with anything, Mr Wright?'

'Maybe. Possibly. You interested?'

'Yes, sir.'

'The police chief down at Deming needed to get rid of me for a spell.'

'Why, Mr Wright?'

'Well, because folks was askin' questions about that robbery an' the money. They come out to my ranch an' tried to prod me into doin' somethin'. The police chief came out too. The way he told it sure as hell's hot them highwaymen headed north . . . I took 'em up on it. After I got here things commenced happenin'. You'n me talked. The robbers had got shot up an' it began to seem like I got talked into ridin' a wrong trail. Marshal, I'll be on the southbound stage in the mornin'. I'm real grateful for all you did.' Carl Wright leaned back so the platter wouldn't be interfered with and went to eating. Sherm finished first, arose, spilled silver, gave the large man a light pat and walked out into an increasing afternoon of early shadows.

He went down to Lisbeth's cottage, let himself in, stood in her brother's bedroom door until Al noticed him then sat on the only chair as Lisbeth's brother said, 'I never would've dreamt it.'

'Dreamt what?'

'She's goin' to marry him. Sherm, the three of 'em livin' in that big house out yonder . . . Lisbeth don't know what she's lettin' herself in for . . . but maybe he won't come back.'

'Al, what in the hell are you talkin' about?'

Burton propped himself with considerable care and scowled. 'Lisbeth agreed she'd stand hitched with Will Culley. Travis left on the late day northbound for up north. Denver, I guess. Travellin' light, Lisbeth told me. He done that once years ago, an' didn't come back for a week.'

Sherm folded both arms behind his head and smiled at the injured man. 'He's earned it, Al. Spent most of his ill-begotten life nursin' calves out yonder. He's earned time off.' Sherm lowered the arms and leaned. 'You got reason he might not come back?'

'That's what he told 'em at the saloon.' Burton made a deprecating gesture. 'Saloon talk. Years back my pa said if a man waited long enough he'd hear anythin' he wanted to hear in a saloon.'

Sherm asked where Lisbeth was and got a reply that brought him to his feet. 'Said somethin' about visitin' your jailhouse ... about an hour ago. Sherm? I thought you might marry her.'

The marshal was heading for the parlour when he replied, 'I thought so too for a spell. You're lookin' better, Al.'

The roadway door noisily closed before Sherm got it all out. 'I figured I might, some day.'

Before he reached the jailhouse he encountered Lisbeth across the road out front of Frank Christy's emporium. She waved and crossed toward him.

He held the door open for her and closed it after she was inside.

She sat on the wall bench, fished for her little wadded handkerchief and said, 'Will asked if I'd marry him.'

'An' you said you would.'

Lisbeth's cheeks got a light shade of pink. 'I did. You like him, don't you?'

'I've liked him since I first came here.' Sherm showed a weak smile. 'Do you expect Travis will come back?'

Lisbeth said, 'I don't. From what Will's mother told me years ago . . . he won't.'

'How much will that stirrup fetch him, Lisbeth?'

She faintly shrugged. 'I got to guess. Enough for him to buy another place somewhere.' She arose. 'Al'll need feedin'. He gets as mean as a hornet.'

'You spoilt him, Lisbeth.'

She stopped at the door. 'You know what he figured to do? Start a freight an' stage company here in Culleyville.'

Sherm chuckled. 'Gettin' shot in the . . . well, close to it — does things to men. Lisbeth? Keep him home. He'll make a good worker.'

After she departed, Sherm dumped his hat, groped low, took the bottle to the chair with him, sat down, worried loose the cork with his teeth and got two swallows down before Pansy Christy came, smiling so wide it must have hurt. She ignored the bottle, sat where the wall bench was probably still warm and said, 'Pa says there's the marryin' kind and the not marryin' kind . . . he said for me to ask which you are.'

'The unmarryin' kind, Pansy.'

'Mind if I have a nip?' she said, and

reached for the bottle.

She, too, swallowed twice, smoothed her dress and hesitated with the drawstring in her dimpled fat hand. 'In a couple of years, Sherm.'

He agreed. 'That'd maybe be about the right time.'

He waited until the last echo died then tucked the bottle away and locked up from the outside before crossing over and going no further than the saloon. It was getting along toward dusk and he had an arduous long day planned for tomorrow. He knew where that high-up narrow opening was in the red rock.

THE END